W9-ADI-989

24

LINDA TRESSEL

ANTHONY TROLLOPE, the fourth of six surviving children, was born on 24 April 1815 in London. As he describes in his *Autobiography*, poverty and debt made his childhood acutely unhappy and disrupted his education: his school fees at Harrow and Winchester were frequently unpaid. His family attempted to restore their fortunes by going to America, leaving the young Anthony alone in England, but it was not until his mother, Frances, began to write that there was any improvement in the family's finances. Her success came too late for her husband, who died in exile in Belgium in 1835. Trollope was unable to afford a university education, and in 1834 he became a junior clerk in the Post Office. He achieved little until he was appointed Surveyor's Clerk in Ireland in 1841. There he worked hard, travelled widely, took up hunting and still found time for his literary career. He married Rose Heseltine, the daughter of a bank manager, in 1844; they had two sons, one of whom emigrated to Australia. Trollope frequently went abroad for the Post Office and did not settle in England again until 1859. He is still remembered as the inventor of the letter-box. In 1867 he resigned from the Post Office and became the editor of *St Paul's Magazine* for the next three years. He failed in his attempt to enter Parliament as a Liberal in 1868. Trollope took his place among London literary society and counted William Thackeray, George Eliot and G. H. Lewes among his friends. He died on 6 December 1882 as the result of a stroke.

Anthony Trollope wrote forty-seven novels and five volumes of short stories as well as travel books, biographies and collections of sketches. The Barsetshire series and the six Palliser or 'political' books were the first novel-sequences to be written in English. His works offer an unsurpassed portrait of the professional and landed classes of Victorian England. In his *Autobiography* (published posthumously in 1883) Trollope describes the self-discipline that enabled his prolific output: he would produce a given number of words per hour in the early morning, before work; he always wrote while travelling by rail or sea, and as soon as he finished one novel he began another. His efforts resulted in his becoming one of England's most successful and popular writers.

Linda Tressel (1868) was published anonymously, with 'By the Author of Nina Balatka' on the title page. Trollope had felt there was often injustice in the critical praise heaped upon established authors while beginners were neglected. As he describes in his *Autobiography*, he determined upon an experiment, 'to begin a course of novels anonymously, in order that I might see whether I could succeed in obtaining a second identity, – whether as I had made one mark by such literary ability as I possessed, I might succeed in doing so again … Another ten years of unpaid unflagging labour might have built up a second reputation … I could not at once induce English readers to read what I gave to them, unless I gave it with my name.' And so, despite some notice by the critics, the experiment was abandoned.

LINDA TRESSEL

ANTHONY TROLLOPE

PENGUIN BOOKS

PENGUIN BOOKS

Published by the Penguin Group
Penguin Books Ltd, 27 Wrights Lane, London W8 5TZ, England
Penguin Books USA Inc., 375 Hudson Street, New York, New York 10014, USA
Penguin Books Australia Ltd, Ringwood, Victoria, Australia
Penguin Books Canada Ltd, 10 Alcorn Avenue, Toronto, Ontario, Canada M4V 3B2
Penguin Books (NZ) Ltd, 182–190 Wairau Road, Auckland 10, New Zealand

Penguin Books Ltd, Registered Offices: Harmondsworth, Middlesex, England

First published 1868
Published in Penguin Books 1993
1 3 5 7 9 10 8 6 4 2

Printed in England by Clays Ltd, St Ives plc

THE PERSONS OF THE STORY

HERR MOLK — *A Magistrate at Nuremberg.*

PETER STEINMARC — *Town-Clerk to the City Magistrates.*

MADAME STAUBACH — *A Widow living in the Red House.*

LINDA TRESSEL — *Her Niece.*

LUDOVIC VALCARM — *A Young Man of Nuremberg, cousin to Steinmarc.*

JACOB HEISSE — *An Upholsterer at Nuremberg.*

FANNY HEISSE — *His Daughter—afterwards married to Max Bogen.*

TETCHEN — *Servant to Madame Staubach.*

STOBE — *A Brewer's Hacker.*

MAX BOGEN — *A Young Lawyer of Augsburg.*

CHAPTER I

THE troubles and sorrows of Linda Tressel, who is the heroine of the little story now about to be told, arose from the too rigid virtue of her nearest and most loving friend,—as troubles will sometimes come from rigid virtue when rigid virtue is not accompanied by sound sense, and especially when it knows little or nothing of the softness of mercy.

The nearest and dearest friend of Linda Tressel was her aunt, the widow Staubach—Madame Charlotte Staubach, as she had come to be called in the little town of Nuremberg where she lived. In Nuremberg all houses are picturesque, but you shall go through the entire city and find no more picturesque abode than the small red house with the three gables close down by the river-side in the Schütt island—the little island made by the river Pegnitz in the middle of the town. They who have seen the widow Staubach's house will have remembered it, not only because of its bright colour and its sharp gables, but also because of the garden which runs between the house and the water's edge. And yet the garden was no bigger than may often nowadays be seen in the balconies of the mansions of Paris and of London. Here Linda Tressel lived with her aunt, and here also Linda had been born.

Linda was the orphan of Herr Tressel, who had for many years been what we may call town-clerk to the magistrates of Nuremberg. Chance in middle life had taken him to Cologne—a German city indeed, as was his own, but a city so far away from Nuremberg that its people and its manners were as strange to him as though he had gone beyond the reach of his own mother-tongue. But here he had married, and from Cologne had brought home his bride to the picturesque, red, gabled house by the water's side in his own city. His wife's only sister had also married, in her own town; and that sister was the virtuous but rigid aunt Charlotte, to live with whom had been the fate in life of Linda Tressel.

It need not be more than told in the fewest words that the town-clerk and the town-clerk's wife both died when Linda was but an infant, and that the husband of her aunt Charlotte died also. In Nuremberg there is no possession so much coveted and so dearly loved as that of the house in which the family lives. Herr Tressel had owned the house with the three gables, and so had his father before him, and to the father it had come from an uncle whose name had been different,—and to him from some other relative. But it was an old family property, and, like other houses in Nuremberg, was to be kept in the hands of the family while the family might remain, unless some terrible ruin should supervene.

When Linda was but six years old, her aunt, the widow, came to Nuremberg to inhabit the house which the Tressels had left as an only legacy to their daughter; but it was understood when she did so that a right of living in the house for the remainder of her days was to belong to Madame Staubach because of the surrender she thus made of whatever of a home was then left to her in Cologne. There was probably no deed executed to this effect; nor would it have been thought that any deed was necessary. Should Linda Tressel, when years had rolled on, be taken as a wife, and should the husband live in the red house, there would still be room for Linda's aunt. And by no husband in Nuremberg, who should be told that such an arrangement had been anticipated, would such an arrangement be opposed. Mothers-in-law, aunts, maiden sisters, and dependent female relatives, in all degrees, are endured with greater patience and treated with a gentler hand in patient Bavaria than in some lands farther west where life is faster, and in which men's shoulders are more easily galled by slight burdens. And as poor little Linda Tressel had no other possession but the house, as all other income, slight as it might be, was to be brought with her by aunt Charlotte, aunt Charlotte had at least a right to the free use of the roof over her head. It is necessary that so much should be told; but Linda's troubles did not come from the divided right which she had in her father's house. Linda's troubles, as has before been said, sprang not from her aunt's covetousness, but from her aunt's virtue—perhaps we might more truly say, from her aunt's religion.

Nuremberg is one of those German cities in which a stranger finds it difficult to understand the religious idiosyncrasies of the people. It is in Bavaria, and Bavaria, as he knows, is Roman Catholic. But Nuremberg is Protestant, and the stranger, when he visits the two cathedrals—those of St. Sebald and St. Lawrence—finds it hard to believe that they should not be made to resound with masses, so like are they in all respects to other Romanist cathedrals which he has seen. But he is told that they are Lutheran and Protestant, and he is obliged to make himself aware that the prevailing religion of Nuremberg is Lutheran, in spite of what to him are the Catholic appearances of the churches. Now the widow Staubach was among Protestants the most Protestant, going far beyond the ordinary amenities of Lutheran teaching, as at present taught, in her religious observances, her religious loves, and her religious antipathies. The ordinary Lutheran of the German cities does not wear his religion very conspicuously. It is not a trouble to him in his daily life, causing him to live in terror as to the life to come. That it is a comfort to him let us not doubt. But it has not on him generally that outward, ever palpable, unmistakable effect, making its own of his gait, his countenance, his garb, his voice, his words, his eyes, his thoughts, his clothes, his very sneeze, his cough, his sighs, his groans, which is the result of Calvinistic impressions thoroughly brought home to the mind and lovingly entertained in the heart. Madame Staubach was in truth a German Anabaptist, but it will be enough for us to say that her manners and gait were the manners and gait of a Calvinist.

While Linda Tressel was a child she hardly knew that her aunt was peculiar in her religious ideas. That mode of life which comes to a child comes naturally, and Linda, though she was probably not allowed to play as freely as did the other bairns around her, though she was taken more frequently to the house of worship which her aunt

frequented, and targed more strictly in the reading of
godly books, did not know till she was a child no longer,
that she was subjected to harder usage than others endured. But when Linda was eleven, the widow was persuaded by a friend that it was her duty to send her niece
to school; and when Linda at sixteen ceased to be a school
girl, she had learned to think that the religion of her
aunt's neighbours was a more comfortable religion than
that practised by her aunt; and when she was eighteen,
she had further learned to think that the life of certain
neighbour girls was a pleasanter life than her own. When
she was twenty, she had studied the subject more deeply,
and had told herself that though her spirit was prone to
rebel against her aunt, that though she would fain have
been allowed to do as did other girls of twenty, yet she
knew her aunt to be a good woman, and knew that it
behoved her to obey. Had not her aunt come all the way
from Cologne, from the distant city of Rhenish Prussia,
to live in Nuremberg for her sake, and should she be un-
faithful and rebellious? Now Madame Staubach understood and appreciated the proneness to rebellion in her
niece's heart, but did not quite understand, and perhaps
could not appreciate, the attempt to put down that rebellion which the niece was ever making from day to
day.

I have said that the widow Staubach had brought with
her to Nuremberg some income upon which to live in the
red house with the three gables. Some small means of her
own she possessed, some few hundred florins a-year, which
were remitted to her punctually from Cologne; but this
would not have sufficed even for the moderate wants of
herself, her niece, and of the old maid Tetchen, who
lived with them, and who had lived with Linda's mother.
But there was a source of income very ready to the widow's
hand, and of which it was a matter of course that she
should in her circumstances avail herself. She and her
niece could not fill the family home, and a portion of it
was let to a lodger. This lodger was Herr Steinmarc—
Peter Steinmarc, who had been clerk to Linda's father
when Linda's father had been clerk to the city magistrates,

and who was now clerk to the city magistrates himself. Peter Steinmarc in the old days had inhabited a garret in the house, and had taken his meals at his master's table; but now the first floor of the house was his own, the big airy pleasant chamber looking out from under one gable on to the clear water, and the broad passage under the middle gable, and the square large bedroom—the room in which Linda had been born—under the third gable. The windows from these apartments all looked out on to the slow-flowing but clear stream, which ran so close below them that the town-clerk might have sat and fished from his windows had he been so minded; for there was no road there—only the narrow slip of a garden no broader than a balcony. And opposite, beyond the river, where the road ran, there was a broad place,—the Ruden Platz; and every house surrounding this was picturesque with different colours, and with many gables, and the points of the houses rose up in sharp pyramids, of which every brick and every tile was in its place, sharp, clear, well formed, and appropriate, in those very inches of space which each was called upon to fill. For in Nuremberg it is the religion of the community that no house shall fall into decay, that no form of city beauty shall be allowed to vanish, that nothing of picturesque antiquity shall be changed. From age to age, though stones and bricks are changed, the buildings are the same, and the medieval forms remain, delighting the taste of the traveller as they do the pride of the burgher. Thus it was that Herr Steinmarc, the clerk of the magistrates in Nuremberg, had for his use as pleasant an abode as the city could furnish him.

Now it came to pass that, during the many years of their residence beneath the same roof, there grew up a strong feeling of friendship between Peter Steinmarc and the widow Staubach, so strong that in most worldly matters the widow would be content to follow her friend Peter's counsels without hesitation. And this was the case although Peter by no means lived in accordance with the widow's tenets as to matters of religion. It is not to be understood that Peter was a godless man,—not so especi-

ally, or that he lived a life in any way scandalous, or open
to special animadversion from the converted; but he was
a man of the world, very fond of money, very fond of
business, doing no more in the matter of worship than
is done ordinarily by men of the world,—one who would
not scruple to earn a few gulden on the Sunday if such
earning came in his way, who liked his beer and his pipe,
and, above all things, liked the fees and perquisites of
office on which he lived and made his little wealth. But
though thus worldly he was esteemed much by Madame
Staubach, who rarely, on his behalf, put forth that voice
of warning which was so frequently heard by her niece.

But there are women of the class to which Madame
Staubach belonged who think that the acerbities of religion are intended altogether for their own sex. That
men ought to be grateful to them who will deny? Such
women seem to think that Heaven will pardon that hardness of heart which it has created in man, and which the
affairs of the world seem almost to require; but that it
will extend no such forgiveness to the feminine creation.
It may be necessary that a man should be stiff-necked,
self-willed, eager on the world, perhaps even covetous
and given to worldly lusts. But for a woman, it behoves
her to crush herself, so that she may be at all points submissive, self-denying, and much-suffering. She should be
used to thorns in the flesh, and to thorns in the spirit too.
Whatever may be the thing she wants, that thing she
should not have. And if it be so that, in her feminine
weakness, she be not able to deny herself, there should
be those around her to do the denial for her. Let her crush
herself as it becomes a poor female to do, or let there be
some other female to crush her if she lack the strength,
the purity, and the religious fervour which such self-
crushing requires. Poor Linda Tressel had not much
taste for crushing herself, but Providence had supplied
her with one who had always been willing to do that
work for her. And yet the aunt had ever dearly loved her
niece, and dearly loved her now in these days of our story.
If your eye offend you, shall you not pluck it out?
After a sort Madame Staubach was plucking out her own

eye when she led her niece such a life of torment as will be described in these pages.

When Linda was told one day by Tetchen the old servant that there was a marriage on foot between Herr Steinmarc and aunt Charlotte, Linda expressed her disbelief in very strong terms. When Tetchen produced many arguments to show why it should be so, and put aside as of no avail all the reasons given by Linda to show that such a marriage could hardly be intended, Linda was still incredulous. 'You do not know aunt Charlotte, Tetchen;—not as I do.' said Linda.

'I've lived in the same house with her for fourteen years,' said Tetchen, angrily.

'And yet you do not know her. I am sure she will not marry Peter Steinmarc. She will never marry anybody. She does not think of such things.'

'Pooh!' said Tetchen; 'all women think of them. Their heads are always together, and Peter talks as though he meant to be master of the house, and he tells her everything about Ludovic. I heard them talking about Ludovic for the hour together the other night.'

'You shouldn't listen, Tetchen.'

'I didn't listen, miss. But when one is in and out one cannot stop one's ears. I hope there isn't going to be anything wrong between 'em about the house.'

'My aunt will never do anything wrong, and my aunt will never marry Peter Steinmarc.' So Linda declared in her aunt's defence, and in her latter assertion she was certainly right. Madame Staubach was not minded to marry Herr Steinmarc; but she might have done so had she wished it, for Herr Steinmarc asked her to take him more than once.

At this time the widow Staubach was a woman not much over forty years of age; and though it can hardly be said she was comely, yet she was not without a certain prettiness which might have charms in the judgment of Herr Steinmarc. She was very thin, and her face was pale, and here and there was the beginning of a wrinkle telling as much of trouble as of years; but her eyes were bright and clear, and her smooth hair, of which but the

edge was allowed to be seen beneath her cap, was of as
rich a brown as when she had married Gasper Staubach,
now more than twenty years ago; and her teeth were
white and perfect, and the oval of her face had not been
impaired by time, and her step, though slow, was light
and firm, and her voice, though sad, was low and soft.
In talking to men—to such a man as was Herr Steinmarc—her voice was always low and soft, though there
would be a sharp note in it now and again when she
would be speaking to Tetchen or her niece. Whether it
was her gentle voice, or her bright eyes, or the edge of
soft brown hair beneath her cap, or some less creditable
feeling of covetousness in regard to the gabled house in
the Schütt island, shall not here be even guessed; but it
was the fact that Herr Steinmarc had more than once
asked Madame Staubach to be his wife when Tetchen
first imparted her suspicion to Linda.

'And what were they saying about Ludovic?' asked
Linda, when Tetchen, for the third time came to Linda
with her tidings. Now Linda had scolded Tetchen for
listening to her aunt's conversation about Ludovic, and
Tetchen thought it unjust that she should be interrogated
on the subject after being so treated.

'I told you, miss, I didn't hear anything;—only just
the name.'

'Very well, Tetchen; that will do; only I hope you
won't say such things of aunt Charlotte anywhere else.'

'What harm have I said, Linda? surely to say of a
widow that she's to be married to an honest man is not
to say harm.'

'But it is not true, Tetchen; and you should not say it.'
Then Tetchen departed quite unconvinced, and Linda
began to reflect how far her life would be changed for
the better or for the worse, if Tetchen's tidings should
ever be made true. But, as has been said before, Tetchen's
tidings were never to be made true.

But Madame Staubach did not resent the offer made
to her. When Peter Steinmarc told her that she was a
lone woman, left without guidance or protection, she
allowed the fact, admitting that guidance would be good

for her. When he went on to say that Linda also was in
need of protection, she admitted that also. 'She is in sore
need,' Madame Staubach said, 'the poor thoughtless
child.' And when Herr Steinmarc spoke of her pecuniary
condition, reminding the widow that were she left without the lodger the two women could hardly keep the old
family roof over their head, Madame Staubach acknowledged it all, and perhaps went very suddenly to the true
point by expressing an opinion that everything would be
much better arranged if the house were the property of
Herr Steinmarc himself. 'It isn't good that women should
own houses,' said Madame Staubach; 'it should be enough
for them that they are permitted to use them.' Then
Herr Steinmarc went on to explain that if the widow
would consent to become his wife, he thought he could
so settle things that for their lives, at any rate, the house
should be in his care and management. But the widow
would not consent even to speak of such an arrangement
as possible. She spoke a word, with a tear in her eye, of
the human lord and master who had lived with her for
two happy years, and said another word with some mysti-
cal allusion to a heavenly husband; and after that Herr
Steinmarc felt that he could not plead his cause further
with any hope of success. 'But why should not Linda be
your wife?' said Madame Staubach, as her disappointed
suitor was about to retire.

The idea had never struck the man's mind before, and
now, when the suggestion was made to him, he was for
a while stricken dumb. Why should he not marry Linda
Tressel, the niece; gay, pretty, young, sweet as youth and
prettiness and gaiety could make her, a girl than whom
there was none prettier, none sweeter, in all Nuremberg
—and the real owner, too, of the house in which he lived,
—instead of the aunt, who was neither gay, nor sweet,
nor young; who, though she was virtuous, self-denying,
and meek, possessed certainly but few feminine charms?
Herr Steinmarc, though he was a man not by any means
living outside the pale of the Church to which he belonged, was not so strongly given to religious observances
as to have preferred the aunt because of her piety and

sanctity of life. He was not hypocrite enough to suggest to Madame Staubach that any such feeling warmed his bosom. Why should not Linda be his wife? He sat himself down again in the arm-chair from which he had risen, and began to consider the question.

In the first place, Herr Steinmarc was at this time nearly fifty years old, and Linda Tressel was only twenty. He knew Linda's age well, for he had been an inhabitant of the garret up-stairs when Linda was born. What would the Frau Tressel have said that night had any one prophesied to her that her little daughter would hereafter be offered as a wife to her husband's penniless clerk up-stairs? But penniless clerks often live to fill their masters' shoes, and do sometimes marry their masters' daughters. And then Linda was known throughout Nuremberg to be the real owner of the house with the three gables, and Herr Steinmarc had an idea that the Nuremberg magistrates would rise up against him were he to offer to marry the young heiress. And there was a third difficulty: Herr Steinmarc, though he had no knowledge on the subject, though his suspicions were so slight that he had never mentioned them to his old friend the widow, though he was aware that he had barely a ground for the idea, still had an idea, that Linda Tressel's heart was no longer at Linda's own disposal.

But nevertheless the momentous question which had been so suddenly asked him was one which certainly deserved the closest consideration. It showed him, at any rate, that Linda's nearest friend would help him were he inclined to prosecute such a suit, and that she saw nothing out of course, nothing anomalous, in the proposition. It would be very nice to be the husband of a pretty, gay, sweet-tempered, joyous young girl. It would be very nice to marry the heiress of the house, and to become its actual owner and master, and it would be nice also to be preferred to him of whom Peter Steinmarc had thought as the true possessor of Linda's heart. If Linda were once his wife, Linda, he did not doubt, would be true to him. In such case Linda, whom he knew to be a good girl, would overcome any little prejudice of her girlhood. Other men of fifty had married girls of twenty, and why should not he, Peter Steinmarc, the well-to-do, comfortable, and, considering his age, good-looking town-clerk of the city of Nuremberg? He could not bring himself to tell Madame Staubach that he would transfer his affections to her niece on that occasion on which the question was first asked. He would take a week, he said, to consider. He took the week; but made up his mind on the first day of the week, and at the end of the week declared to Madame Staubach that he thought the plan to be a good plan.

After that there was much discussion before any further step was taken, and Tetchen was quite sure that their lodger was to be married to Linda's aunt. There was much discussion, and the widow, shocked, perhaps, at her own cruelty, almost retreated from the offer she had made. But Herr Steinmarc was emboldened, and was now eager, and held her to her own plan. It was a good plan, and he was ready. He found that he could love the maiden, and he wished to take her to his bosom at once. For a few days the widow's heart relented; for a few days there came across her breast a frail, foolish, human idea of love and passion, and the earthly joy of two young beings, happy in each other's arms. For a while she thought with regret of what she was about to do, of the sacrifice to be made, of the sorrow to be endured, of the deathblow to be given to those dreams of love, which doubtless had arisen, though hitherto they were no more than dreams. Madame Staubach, though she was now a saint, had been once a woman, and knew as well as any woman of what nature are the dreams of love which fill the heart of a girl. It was because she knew them so well, that she allowed herself only a few hours of such weakness. What! should she hesitate between heaven and hell, between God and devil, between this world and the next, between sacrifice of time and sacrifice of eternity, when the disposal of her own niece, her own child, her nearest and dearest, was concerned? Was it not fit that the world should be crushed in the bosom of a young girl? and how could it be crushed so effectually as by marrying her to an old man, one whom she respected, but who was otherwise distasteful to her— one who, as a husband, would at first be abhorrent to her? As Madame Staubach thought of heaven then, a girl who loved and was allowed to indulge her love could hardly go to heaven. 'Let it be so,' she said to Peter Steinmarc after a few days of weak vacillation,—'let it be so. I think that it will be good for her.' Then Peter Steinmarc swore that it would be good for Linda—that it should be good for Linda. His care should be so great that Linda might never doubt the good. 'Peter Steinmarc, I am thinking of her soul,' said Madame Staubach. 'I am thinking of that too,' said Peter; 'one has, you know, to think of everything in turns.'

Then there came to be a little difficulty as to the manner in which the proposition should be first made to Linda Tressel. Madame Staubach thought that it should be made by Peter himself, but Peter was of opinion that if the ice were first broken by Madame Staubach, final success might be more probably achieved. 'She owes you obedience, my friend, and she owes me none, as yet,' said Peter. There seemed to be so much of truth in this that Madame Staubach yielded, and undertook to make the first overture to Linda on behalf of her lover.

CHAPTER II

LINDA TRESSEL was a tall, light-built, active young woman, in full health, by no means a fine lady, very able and very willing to assist Tetchen in the work of the house, or rather to be assisted by Tetchen in doing it, and fit at all points to be the wife of any young burgher in Nuremberg. And she was very pretty withal, with eager, speaking eyes, and soft luxurious tresses, not black, but of so very dark a brown as to be counted black in some lights. It was her aunt's care to have these tresses confined, so that nothing of their wayward obstinacy in curling might be seen by the eyes of men; and Linda strove to obey her aunt, but the curls would sometimes be too strong for Linda, and would be seen over her shoulders and across her back, tempting the eyes of men sorely. Peter Steinmarc had so seen them many a time, and thought much of them when the offer of Linda's hand was first made to him. Her face, like that of her aunt, was oval in its form, and her complexion was dark and clear. But perhaps her greatest beauty consisted in the half-soft, half-wild expression of her face, which, while it seemed to declare to the world that she was mild, gentle, and, for the most part, silent, gave a vague, doubtful promise of something that might be beyond, if only her nature were sufficiently awakened, creating a hope and mysterious longing for something more than might be expected from a girl brought up under the severe thraldom of Madame Charlotte Staubach,—creating a hope, or perhaps it might be a fear. And Linda's face in this respect was the true reflex of her character. She lived with her aunt a quiet, industrious, sober life, striving to be obedient, striving to be religious with the religion of her aunt. She had almost brought herself to believe that it was good for her heart to be crushed. She had quite brought herself to wish to believe it. She had within her heart no desire for open rebellion against domestic authority. The world was a dangerous, bad world, in which men were dust and women something lower than dust. She would tell herself so very often, and strive to believe herself when she did so. But, for all this, there was a yearning for something beyond her present life, for something that should be of the world, worldly. When she heard profane music she would long to dance. When she heard the girls laughing in the public gardens she would long to stay and laugh with them. Pretty ribbons and bright-coloured silks were a snare to her. When she could shake out her curly locks in the retirement of her own little chamber, she liked to feel them and to know that they were pretty.

But these were the wiles with which the devil catches the souls of women, and there were times when she believed that the devil was making an especial struggle to possess himself of her. There were moments in which she almost thought that the devil would succeed, and that, perhaps, it was but of little use for her to carry on any longer the futile contest. Would it not be pleasant to give up the contest, and to laugh and talk and shout and be merry, to dance, and wear bright colours, and be gay in company with young men, as did the other girls around her? As for those other girls, their elder friends did not seem on their account to be specially in dread of Satan. There was Fanny Heisse who lived close to them, who had been Linda's friend when they went to school together. Fanny did just as she pleased, was always talking with young men, wore the brightest ribbons that the shops produced, was always dancing, seemed to be bound by no strict rules on life; and yet everybody spoke well of Fanny Heisse, and now Fanny was to be married to a young lawyer from Augsburg. Could it be the fact that the devil had made sure of Fanny Hèisse? Linda had been very anxious to ask her aunt a question on that subject, but had been afraid. Whenever she attempted to discuss any point of theology with her aunt, such attempts always ended in renewed assurances of the devil's greediness, and in some harder, more crushing rule by which the devil's greed might be outwitted.

Then there came a time of terrible peril, and poor Linda was in greater doubt than ever. Fanny Heisse, who was to be married to the Augsburg lawyer, had long been accustomed to talk to young men, to one young man after another, so that young men had come to be almost nothing to her. She had selected one as her husband because it had been suggested to her that she had better settle herself in life; and this special one was well-to-do, and good-looking, and pleasant-mannered, and good-tempered. The whole thing with Fanny Heisse had seemed to go as though flirting, love, and marriage all came naturally, without danger, without care, and without disappointment. But a young man had now spoken to her, to Linda,—had spoken to her words that she did not dare to repeat to any one,—had spoken to her twice, thrice, and she had not rebuked him. She had not, at least, rebuked him with that withering scorn which the circumstances had surely required, and which would have made him know that she regarded him as one sent purposely from the Evil One to tempt her. Now again had come upon her some terrible half-formed idea that it would be well to give up the battle and let the Evil One make free with his prey. But, in truth, her heart within her had so palpitated with emotion when these words had been spoken and been repeated, that she had lacked the strength to carry on the battle properly. How send a daring young man from you with withering scorn, when there lacks power to raise the eyes, to open or to close the lips, to think even at the moment whether such scorn is deserved, or something very different from scorn?

The young man had not been seen by Linda's eyes for nearly a month, when Peter Steinmarc and Madam Staubach settled between them that the ice should be broken. On the following morning aunt Charlotte prepared herself for the communication to be made, and, when she came in from her market purchases, went at once to her task. Linda was found by her aunt in their lodger's sitting-room, busy with brooms and brushes, while Tetchen on her knees was dry-rubbing the polished board round the broad margin of the room. 'Linda,' said Madame Staubach, 'I have that which I wish to say to you; would you come with me for a while?' Then Linda followed her aunt to Madame Staubach's own chamber, and as she went there came over her a guilty fear. Could it be that her aunt had heard of the words which the young man had spoken to her?

'Linda,' said Madame Staubach, 'sit down,—there, in my chair. I have a proposition to make to you of much importance,—of very great importance. May the Lord grant that the thing that I do shall be right in His sight!'

'To make to me, aunt?' said Linda, now quite astray as to her aunt's intention. She was sure, at least, that there was no danger about the young man. Had it been her aunt's purpose to rebuke her for aught that she had done, her aunt's manner and look would have been very different,—would have been hard, severe, and full of denunciation. As it was, Madame Staubach almost hesitated in her words, and certainly had assumed much less than her accustomed austerity.

'I hope, Linda, that you know that I love you.'

'I am sure that you love me, aunt Charlotte. But why do you ask me?'

'If there be any one in this world that I do love, it is you, my child. Who else is there left to me? Were it not for you, the world with all its troubles would be nothing to me, and I could prepare myself to go in peace when He should be pleased to take me.'

'But why do you say this now, aunt Charlotte?'

'I will tell you why I say it now. Though I am hardly an old woman yet——'

'Of course you are not an old woman.'

'I wish I were older, that I might be nearer to my rest. But you are young, and it is necessary that your future life should be regarded. Whether I go hence or remain here it will be proper that some settlement should be made for you.' Then Madame Staubach paused, and Linda began to think that her aunt had on her mind some scheme about the house. When her aunt had spoken of going hence or remaining here, Linda had not been quite sure whether the goings and remainings spoken of were wholly spiritual or whether there was any reference to things worldly and temporal. Could it be that Tetchen was after all right in her surmise? Was it possible that her aunt was about to be married to Peter Steinmarc? But she said nothing; and after a while her aunt went on very slowly with her proposition. 'Yes, Linda, some settlement for your future life should be made. You know that the house in which we live is your own.'

'It is yours and mine together, aunt.'

'No, Linda; the house is your own. And the furniture in it is yours too; so that Herr Steinmarc is your lodger. It is right that you should understand all this; but I think too well of my own child to believe that she will ever on that account be disobedient or unruly.'

'That will never make a difference.'

'No, Linda; I am sure it will not. Providence has been

pleased to put me in the place of both father and mother to you. I will not say that I have done my duty by you——'

'You have, aunt, always,' said Linda, taking her aunt's hand and pressing it affectionately.

'But I have found, and I expect to find, a child's obedience. It is good that the young should obey their elders, and should understand that those in authority over them should know better than they can do themselves what is good for them.' Linda was now altogether astray in her thoughts and anticipations. Her aunt had very frequently spoken to her in this strain; nay, a week did not often pass by without such a speech. But then the speeches would come without the solemn prelude which had been made on this occasion, and would be caused generally by some act or word or look or movement on the part of Linda of which Madame Staubach had found herself obliged to express disapprobation. On the present occasion the conversation had been commenced without any such expression. Her aunt had even deigned to commend the general tenor of her life. She had dropped the hand as soon as her aunt began to talk of those in authority, and waited with patience till the gist of the lecture should be revealed to her. 'I hope you will understand this now, Linda. That which I shall propose to you is for your welfare, here and hereafter, even though it may not at first seem to you to be agreeable.'

'What is it, aunt?' said Linda, jumping up quickly from her seat.

'Sit down, my child, and I will tell you.' But Linda did not reseat herself at once. Some terrible fear had come upon her,—some fear of she knew not what,—and she found it to be almost impossible to remain quiet at her aunt's knee. 'Sit down, Linda, when I ask you.' Then Linda did sit down; but she had altogether lost that look of quiet, passive endurance which her face and figure had borne when she was first asked to listen to her aunt's words. 'The time in your life has come, my dear, when I as your guardian have to think whether it is not well that you should be—married.'

'But I do not want to be married,' said Linda, jumping up again.

'My dearest child, it would be better that you should listen to me. Marriage, you know, is an honourable state.'

'Yes, I know, of course. But, aunt Charlotte——'

'Hush, my dear.'

'A girl need not be married unless she likes.'

'If I were dead, with whom would you live? Who would there be to guard you and guide you?'

'But you are not going to die.'

'Linda, that is very wicked.'

'And why can I not guide myself?'

'Because you are young, and weak, and foolish. Because it is right that they who are frail, and timid, and spiritless, should be made subject to those who are strong and able to hold dominion and to exact obedience.' Linda did not at all like being told that she was spiritless. She thought that she might be able to show spirit enough were it not for the duty that she owed to her aunt. And as for obedience, though she were willing to obey her aunt, she felt that her aunt had no right to transfer her privilege in that respect to another. But she said nothing, and her aunt went on with her proposition.

'Our lodger, Peter Steinmarc, has spoken to me, and he is anxious to make you his wife.'

'Peter Steinmarc!'

'Yes, Linda; Peter Steinmarc.'

'Old Peter Steinmarc!'

'He is not old. What has his being old to do with it?'

'I will never marry Peter Steinmarc, aunt Charlotte.'

Madame Staubach had not expected to meet with immediate and positive obedience. She had thought it probable that there might be some opposition shown to her plan when it was first brought forward. Indeed, how could it be otherwise, when marriage was suggested abruptly to such a girl as Linda Tressel, even though the suggested husband had been an Apollo? What young woman could have said, 'Oh, certainly; whenever you please, aunt Charlotte,' to such a proposition? Feeling this, Madame Staubach would have gone to work by degrees,—would have opened her siege by gradual trenches, and have approached the citadel by parallels, before she attempted to take it by storm, had she known anything of the ways and forms of such strategy. But though she knew that there were such ways and forms of strategy among the ungodly, out in the world with the worldly, she had practised none such herself, and knew nothing of the mode in which they should be conducted. On this subject, if on any, her niece owed to her obedience, and she would claim that obedience as hers of right. Though Linda would at first be startled, she would probably be not the less willing to obey at last, if she found her guardian stern and resolute in her demand. 'My dear,' she said, 'you have probably not yet had time to think of the marriage which I have proposed to you.'

'I want no time to think of it.'

'Nothing in life should be accepted or rejected without thinking, Linda,—nothing except sin; and thinking cannot be done without time.'

'This would be sin—a great sin!'

'Linda, you are very wicked.'

'Of course, I am wicked.'

'Herr Steinmarc is a most respectable man. There is no man in all Nuremberg more respected than Herr Steinmarc.' This was doubtless Madame Staubach's opinion of Peter Steinmarc, but it may be that Madame Staubach was not qualified to express the opinion of the city in general on that subject. 'He holds the office which your father held before him, and for many years has inhabited the best rooms in your father's house.'

'He is welcome to the rooms if he wants them,' said Linda. 'He is welcome to the whole house if you choose to give it to him.'

'That is nonsense, Linda. Herr Steinmarc wants nothing that is not his of right.'

'I am not his of right,' said Linda.

'Will you listen to me? You are much mistaken if you think that it is because of your trumpery house that this honest man wishes to make you his wife.' We must suppose that Madame Staubach suffered some qualm of conscience as she proffered this assurance, and that she repented afterwards of the sin she committed in making a statement which she could hardly herself have believed to be exactly true. 'He knew your father before you were born, and your mother; and he has known me for many years. Has he not lived with us ever since you can remember?'

'Yes,' said Linda; 'I remember him ever since I was a very little girl,—as long as I can remember anything,— and he seemed to be as old then as he is now.'

'And why should he not be old? Why should you want a husband to be young and foolish and headstrong as you are yourself;—perhaps some one who would drink and gamble and go about after strange women?'

'I don't want any man for a husband,' said Linda.

'There can be nothing more proper than that Herr Steinmarc should make you his wife. He has spoken to me and he is willing to undertake the charge.'

'The charge!' almost screamed Linda, in terrible disgust.

'He is willing to undertake the charge, I say. We shall then still live together, and may hope to be able to maintain a God-fearing household, in which there may be as little opening to the temptations of the world as may be found in any well-ordered house.'

'I do not believe that Peter Steinmarc is a God-fearing man.'

'Linda, you are very wicked to say so.'

'But if he were, it would make no difference.'

'Linda!'

'I only know that he loves his money better than anything in the world, and that he never gives a kreutzer to any one, and that he won't subscribe to the hospital, and he always thinks that Tetchen takes his wine, though Tetchen never touches a drop.'

'When he has a wife she will look after these things.'

'I will never look after them,' said Linda.

The conversation was brought to an end as soon after this as Madame Staubach was able to close it. She had done all that she had intended to do, and had done it with as much of good result as she had expected. She had probably not thought that Linda would be quite so fierce as she had shown herself; but she had expected tears, and more of despair, and a clearer protestation of abject misery in the proposed marriage. Linda's mind would now be filled with the idea, and probably she might by degrees reconcile herself to it, and learn to think that Peter was not so very old a man. At any rate it would now be for Peter himself to carry on the battle.

Linda, as soon as she was alone, sat down with her hands before her and with her eyes fixed, gazing on vacancy, in order that she might realise to herself the thing proposed to her. She had said very little to her aunt of the nature of the misery which such a marriage seemed to offer to her,—not because her imagination made for her no clear picture on the subject, not because she did not foresee unutterable wretchedness in such a union. The picture of such wretchedness had been very palpable to her. She thought that no consideration on earth would induce her to take that mean-faced old man to her breast as her husband, her lord—as the one being whom she was to love beyond everybody else in this world. The picture was clear enough, but she had argued to herself, unconsciously, that any description of that picture to her aunt would seem to suppose that the consummation of the picture was possible. She preferred therefore to declare that the thing was impossible,—an affair the completion of which would be quite out of the question. Instead of assuring her aunt that it would have made her miserable to have to look after Peter Steinmarc's wine, she at once protested that she never would take upon herself that duty. 'I am not his of right,' she had said; and as she said it, she resolved that she would adhere to that protest. But when she was alone she remembered her aunt's demand, her own submissiveness, her old habits of obedience, and above all she remembered the fear that would come over her that she was giving herself to the devil in casting from her her obedience on such a subject, and then she became very wretched. She told herself that sooner or later her aunt would conquer her, that sooner or later that mean-faced old man, with his snuffy fingers, and his few straggling hairs brushed over his bald pate, with his big shoes spreading here and there because of his corns, and his ugly, loose, square, snuffy coat, and his old hat which he had worn so long that she never liked to touch it, would become her husband, and that it would be her duty to look after his wine, and his old shoes, and his old hat, and to have her own little possessions doled out to her by his penuriousness. Though she continued to swear to herself that heaven and earth together should never make her become Herr Steinmarc's wife, yet at the same time she continued to bemoan the certainty of her coming fate. If they were both against her—both, with the Lord on their sides—how could she stand against them with nothing to aid her,—nothing, but the devil, and a few words spoken to her by one whom hitherto she had never dared to answer?

The house in which Linda and Madame Staubach lived, of which the three gables faced towards the river, and which came so close upon the stream that there was but a margin six feet broad between the wall and the edge of the water, was approached by a narrow street or passage, which reached as far as the end of the house, where there was a small gravelled court or open place, perhaps thirty feet square. Opposite to the door of the red house was the door of that in which lived Fanny Heisse with her father and mother. They indeed had another opening into one of the streets of the town, which was necessary, as Jacob Heisse was an upholsterer, and required an exit from his premises for chairs and tables. But to the red house with the three gables there was no other approach than by the narrow passage which ran between the river and the back of Heisse's workshop. Thus the little courtyard was very private, and Linda could stand leaning on the wicket-gate which divided the little garden from the court, without being subject to the charge of making herself public to the passers-by. Not but what she might be seen when so standing by those in the Ruden Platz on the other side of the river, as had often been pointed out to her by her aunt. But it was a habit with her to stand there, perhaps because while so standing she would often hear the gay laugh of her old friend Fanny, and would thus, at second hand, receive some impress from the gaiety of the world without. Now, in her musing, without thinking much of whither she was going, she went slowly down the stairs and out of the door, and stood leaning upon the gate looking over the river at the men who were working in the front of the warehouses. She had not been there long when Fanny ran across to her from the door of her father's house. Fanny Heisse was a bright broad-faced girl, with light hair, and laughing eyes, and a dimple on her chin, freckled somewhat, with a pug nose, and a large mouth. But for all this Fanny Heisse was known throughout Nuremberg as a pretty girl.

'Linda, what do you think?' said Fanny. 'Papa was at Augsburg yesterday, and has just come home, and it is all to come off the week after next.'

'And you are happy?'

'Of course I'm happy. Why shouldn't a girl be happy? He's a good fellow and deserves it all, and I mean to be such a wife to him! Only he is to let me dance. But you don't care for dancing?'

'I have never tried it—much.'

'No; your people think it wicked. I am so glad mine don't. But, Linda, you'll be let come to my marriage—will you not? I do so want you to come. I was making up the party just now with mother and his sister Marie. Father brought Marie home with him. And we have put you down for one. But, Linda, what ails you? Does anything ail you?' Fanny might well ask, for the tears were running down Linda's face.

'It is nothing particular.'

'Nay, but it is something particular—something very particular. Linda, you mope too much.'

'I have not been moping now. But, Fanny, I cannot talk to you about it. I cannot indeed—not now. Do not be angry with me if I go in and leave you.' Then Linda ran in, and went up to her bedroom and bolted the door.

CHAPTER III

PETER STEINMARC had a cousin in a younger generation than himself, who lived in Nuremberg, and who was named Ludovic Valcarm. The mother of this young man had been Peter's first cousin, and when she died Ludovic had in some sort fallen into the hands of his relative the town-clerk. Ludovic's father was still alive; but he was a thriftless, aimless man, who had never been of service either to his wife or children, and at this moment no one knew where he was living, or what he was doing. No one knew, unless it was his son Ludovic, who never received much encouragement in Nuremberg to talk about his father. At the present moment, Peter Steinmarc and his cousin, though they had not actually quarrelled, were not on the most friendly terms. As Peter, in his younger days, had been clerk to old Tressel, so had Ludovic been brought up to act as clerk to Peter; and for three or four years the young man had received some small modicum of salary from the city chest, as a servant in the employment of the city magistrates. But of late Ludovic had left his uncle's office, and had entered the service of certain brewers in Nuremberg, who were more liberal in their views as to wages than were the city magistrates. Peter Steinmarc had thought ill of his cousin for making this change. He had been at the trouble of pointing out to Ludovic how he himself had in former years sat upon the stool in the office in the town-hall, from whence he had been promoted to the arm-chair; and had almost taken upon himself to promise that the good fortune of Ludovic should be as great as his own, if only Ludovic for the present would be content with the stool. But young Valcarm, who by this time was four-and-twenty, told his cousin very freely that the stool in the town-hall suited him no longer, and that he liked neither the work nor the wages. Indeed, he went further than this, and told his kinsman that he liked the society of the office as little as he did either the wages or the work. It may naturally be supposed that this was not said till there had been some unpleasant words spoken

by the town-clerk to his assistant,—till the authority of
the elder had been somewhat stretched over the head of
the young man; but it may be supposed also that when
such words had once been spoken, Peter Steinmarc did
not again press Ludovic Valcarm to sit upon the official
stool.

Ludovic had never lived in the garret of the red house
as Peter himself had done. When the suggestion that he
should do so had some years since been made to Madame
Staubach, that prudent lady, foreseeing that Linda would
soon become a young woman, had been unwilling to sanction the arrangement. Ludovic, therefore, had housed
himself elsewhere, and had been free of the authority of
the town-clerk when away from his office. But he had
been often in his cousin's rooms, and there had grown
up some acquaintance between him and aunt Charlotte
and Linda. It had been very slight;—so thought aunt
Charlotte. It has been as slight as her precautions could
make it. But Ludovic, nevertheless, had spoken such
words to Linda that Linda had been unable to answer
him; and though Madame Staubach was altogether
ignorant that such iniquity had been perpetrated, Peter
Steinmarc had shrewdly guessed the truth.

Rumours of a very ill sort had reached the red house
respecting Ludovic Valcarm. When Linda had interrogated Tetchen as to the nature of the things that were
said of Ludovic in that conversation between Peter and
Madame Staubach which Tetchen had overheard, she
had not asked without some cause. She knew that evil
things were said of the young man, and that evil words
regarding him had been whispered by Peter into her
aunt's ears;—that such whisperings had been going on
almost ever since the day on which Ludovic had declined to return again to the official stool; and she knew,
she thought that she knew, that such whisperings were not
altogether undeserved. There was a set of young men
in Nuremberg of whom it was said that they had a
bad name among their elders,—that they drank spirits
instead of beer, that they were up late at nights, that
they played cards among themselves, that they were

very unfrequent at any house of prayer, that they
belonged to some turbulent political society which had,
to the grief of all the old burghers, been introduced
into Nuremberg from Munich, that they talked of
women as women are talked of in Paris and Vienna
and other strongholds of iniquity, and that they
despised altogether the old habits and modes of life of
their forefathers. They were known by their dress. They
wore high round hats like chimney-pots,—such as were
worn in Paris,—and satin stocks, and tight-fitting costly
coats of fine cloth, and long pantaloons, and they carried
little canes in their hands, and gave themselves airs, and
were very unlike what the young men of Nuremberg
used to be. Linda knew their appearance well, and
thought that it was not altogether unbecoming. But she
knew also,—for she had often been so told,—that they
were dangerous men, and she was grieved that Ludovic
Valcarm should be among their number.

But now—now that her aunt had spoken to her of that
horrid plan in reference to Peter Steinmarc, what would
Ludovic Valcarm be to her? Not that he could ever
have been anything. She knew that, and had known it
from the first, when she had been unable to answer him
with the scorn which his words had deserved. How
could such a one as she be mated with a man so unsuited
to her aunt's tastes, to her own modes of life, as Ludovic
Valcarm? And yet she could have wished that it might
be otherwise. For a moment once,—perhaps for moments
more than once,—there had been ideas that no mission
could be more fitting for such a one as she than that of
bringing back to the right path such a young man as
Ludovic Valcarm. But then,—how to begin to bring
a young man back? She knew that she would not be
allowed to accept his love; and now,—now that the
horrid plan had been proposed to her, any such scheme
was more impracticable, more impossible than ever. Ah,
how she hated Peter Steinmarc as she thought of all this!

For four or five days after this, not a word was said to
Linda by any one on the hated subject. She kept out of
Peter Steinmarc's way as well as she could, and made

herself busy through the house with an almost frantic
energy. She was very good to her aunt, doing every
behest that was put upon her, and going through her
religious services with a zeal which almost seemed to
signify that she liked them. She did not leave the house
once except in her aunt's company, and restrained herself even from leaning over the wicket-gate and listening
to the voice of Fanny Heisse. There were moments during
these days in which she thought that her opposition to
her aunt's plan had had the desired effect, and that she
was not to be driven mad by the courtship of Peter
Steinmarc. Surely five days would not have elapsed without a word had not the plan been deserted. If that were
the case, how good would she be! If that were the case,
she would resolve, on her aunt's behalf, to be very scorn-
ful to Ludovic Valcarm.

But though she had never gone outside the house without her aunt, though she had never even leaned on the
front wicket, yet she had seen Ludovic. It had been no
fault of hers that he had spied her from the Ruden Platz,
and had kissed his hand to her, and had made a sign to her
which she had only half understood,—by which she had
thought that he had meant to imply that he would come
to her soon. All this came from no fault of hers. She
knew that the centre warehouse in the Ruden Platz opposite belonged to the brewers, Sach Brothers, by whom
Valcarm was employed. Of course it was necessary that
the young man should be among the workmen, who were
always moving barrels about before the warehouse, and
that he should attend to his employers' business. But he
need not have made the sign, or kissed his hand, when
he stood hidden from all eyes but hers beneath the low
dark archway; nor, for the matter of that, need her eyes
have been fixed upon the gateway after she had once
perceived that Ludovic was on the Ruden Platz.

What would happen to her if she were to declare
boldly that she loved Ludovic Valcarm, and intended
to become his wife, and not the wife of old Peter Steinmarc? In the first place, Ludovic had never asked her
to be his wife;—but on that head she had almost no

doubt at all. Ludovic would ask her quickly enough, she was very sure, if only he received sufficient encouragement. And as far as she understood the law of the country in which she lived, no one could, she thought, prevent her from marrying him. In such case she would have a terrible battle with her aunt; but her aunt could not lock her up, nor starve her into submission. It would be very dreadful, and no doubt all good people,—all those whom she had been accustomed to regard as good, —would throw her over and point at her as one abandoned. And her aunt's heart would be broken, and the world,—the world as she knew it,—would pretty nearly collapse around her. Nevertheless she could do it. But were she to do so, would it not simply be that she would have allowed the Devil to get the victory, and that she would have given herself for ever and ever, body and soul, to the Evil One? And then she made a compact with herself,—a compact which she hoped was not a compact with Satan also. If they on one side would not strive to make her marry Peter Steinmarc, she on the other side would say nothing, not a word, to Ludovic Valcarm.

She soon learned, however, that she had not as yet achieved her object by the few words which she had spoken to her aunt. Those words had been spoken on a Monday. On the evening of the following Saturday she sat with her aunt in their own room down-stairs, in the chamber immediately below that occupied by Peter Steinmarc. It was a summer evening in August, and Linda was sitting at the window, with some household needlework in her lap, but engaged rather in watching the warehouse opposite than in sedulous attention to her needle. Her eyes were fixed upon the little doorway, not expecting that any one would be seen there, but full of remembrance of the figure of him who had stood there and had kissed his hand. Her aunt, as was her wont on every Saturday, was leaning over a little table intent on some large book of devotional service, with which she prepared herself for the Sabbath. Close as was her attention now and always to the volume, she

would not on ordinary occasions have allowed Linda's
eyes to stray for so long a time across the river without
recalling them by some sharp word of reproof; but on
this evening she sat and read and said nothing. Either
she did not see her niece, so intent was she on her good
work, or else, seeing her, she chose, for reasons of her
own, to be as one who did not see. Linda was too intent
upon her thoughts to remember that she was sinning
with the sin of idleness, and would have still gazed across
the river had she not heard a heavy footstep in the room
above her head, and the fall of a creaking shoe on the
stairs, a sound which she knew full well, and stump,
bump, dump, Peter Steinmarc was descending from his
own apartments to those of his neighbours below him.
Then immediately Linda withdrew her eyes from the
archway, and began to ply her needle with diligence.
And Madame Staubach looked up from her book, and
became uneasy on her chair. Linda felt sure that Peter
was not going out for an evening stroll, was not in quest
of beer and a friendly pipe at the Rothe Ross. He was
much given to beer and a friendly pipe at the Rothe
Ross; but Linda knew that he would creep down-stairs
somewhat softly when his mind was that way given; not
so softly but what she would hear his steps and know
whither they were wending; but now, from the nature
of the sound, she was quite sure that he was not going
to the inn which he frequented. She threw a hurried
glance round upon her aunt, and was quite sure that her
aunt was of the same opinion. When Herr Steinmarc
paused for half a minute outside her aunt's door, and
then slowly turned the lock, Linda was not a bit surprised; nor was Madame Staubach surprised. She closed
her book with dignity, and sat awaiting the address of
her neighbour.

'Good evening, ladies,' said Peter Steinmarc.

'Good evening, Peter,' said Madame Staubach. It was
many years now since these people had first known each
other, and the town-clerk was always called Peter by his
old friend. Linda spoke not a word of answer to her
lover's salutation.

'It has been a beautiful summer day,' said Peter.

'A lovely day,' said Madame Staubach, 'through the Lord's favour to us.'

'Has the fraulein been out?' asked Peter.

'No; I have not been out,' said Linda, almost savagely.

'I will go and leave you together,' said Madame Staubach, getting up from her chair.

'No, aunt, no,' said Linda. 'Don't go away; pray, do not go away.'

'It is fitting that I should do so,' said Madame Staubach, as with one hand she gently pushed back Linda, who was pressing to the door after her. 'You will stay, Linda, and hear what our friend will say; and remember, Linda, that he speaks with my authority and with my heartfelt prayer that he may prevail.'

'He will never prevail,' said Linda. But neither Madame Staubach nor Peter Steinmarc heard what she said.

Linda had already perceived, perturbed as she was in her mind, that Herr Steinmarc had prepared himself carefully for this interview. He had brought a hat with him into the room, but it was not the hat which had so long been distasteful to her. And he had got on clean bright shoes, as large indeed as the old dirty ones, because Herr Steinmarc was not a man to sacrifice his corns for love; but still shoes that were decidedly intended to be worn only on occasions. And he had changed his ordinary woollen shirt for white linen, and had taken out his new brown frock-coat which he always wore on those high days in Nuremberg on which the magistrates appeared with their civic collars. But, perhaps, the effect which Linda noted most keenly was the debonair fashion in which the straggling hairs had been disposed over the bald pate. For a moment or two a stranger might almost have believed that the pate was not bald.

'My dear young friend,' began the town-clerk, 'your aunt has, I think, spoken to you of my wishes.' Linda muttered something, she knew not what. But though her words were not intelligible, her looks were so, and were not of a kind to have been naturally conducive to much hope in the bosom of Herr Steinmarc. 'Of course, I can understand, Linda, how much this must have taken you by surprise at first. But that surprise will wear off, and I trust that you may gradually come to regard me as your future husband without—without—without anything like fear, you know, or feelings of that kind.' Still she did not speak. 'If you become my wife, Linda, I will do my best to make you always happy.'

'I shall never become your wife, never—never—never.'

'Do not speak so decidedly as that, Linda.'

'I must speak decidedly. I do speak decidedly. I can't speak any other way. You know very well, Herr Steinmarc, that you oughtn't to ask me. It is very wrong of you, and very wicked.'

'Why is it wrong, Linda? Why is it wicked?'

'If you want to get married, you should marry some one as old as yourself.'

'No, Linda, that is not so. It is always thought becoming that the man should be older than the wife.'

'But you are three times as old as I am, and that is not becoming.' This was cruel on Linda's part, and her words also were untrue. Linda would be twenty-one at her next birthday, whereas Herr Steinmarc had not yet reached his fifty-second birthday.

Herr Steinmarc was a man who had a temper of his own, and who was a little touchy on the score of age. Linda knew that he was touchy on the score of age, and had exaggerated her statement with the view of causing pain. It was probably some appreciation of this fact which caused Herr Steinmarc to continue his solicitations with more of authority in his voice than he had hitherto used. 'I am not three times as old as you, Linda; but, whatever may be my age, your aunt, who has the charge of you, thinks that the marriage is a fitting one. You should remember that you cannot fly in her face without committing a great sin. I offer to you an honest household and a respectable position. As Madame Staubach thinks that you should accept them, you must know that you are wrong to answer me with scorn and ribaldry.'

'I have not answered you with ribaldry. It is not ribaldry to say that you are an old man.'

'You have answered me with scorn.'

'I do scorn you, Herr Steinmarc, when you come to me pretending to make love like a young man, with your Sunday clothes on, and your hair brushed smooth, and your new shoes. I do scorn you. And you may go and tell my aunt that I say so, if you like. And as for being an old man, you are an old man. Old men are very well in their way, I daresay; but they shouldn't go about making love to young women.'

Herr Steinmarc had not hoped to succeed on this his first personal venture; but he certainly had not expected to be received after the fashion which Linda had adopted towards him. He had, doubtless, looked very often into Linda's face, and had listened very often to the tone of her voice; but he had not understood what her face expressed, nor had he known what compass that voice would reach. Had he been a wise man,—a man wise as to his own future comfort,—he would have abandoned his present attempt after the lessons which he was now learning. But, as has before been said, he had a temper, and he was now angry with Linda. He was roused, and was disposed to make her know that, old as he was, and bald, and forced to wear awkward shoes, and to stump along heavily, still he could force her to become his wife and to minister to his wants. He understood it all. He knew what were his own deficiencies, and was as wide awake as was Linda herself to the natural desires of a young girl. Madame Staubach was, perhaps, equally awake, but she connected these desires directly with the devil. Because it was natural that a young woman should love a young man, therefore, according to the religious theory of Madame Staubach, it was well that a young woman should marry an old man, so that she might then be crushed and made malleable, and susceptible of that teaching which tells us that all suffering in this world is good for us. Now Peter Steinmarc was by no means alive to the truth of such lessons as these. Religion was all very well. It was an outward sign of a

respectable life,—of a life in which men are trusted and
receive comfortable wages,—and, beyond that, was an
innocent occupation for enthusiastic women. But he had
no idea that any human being was bound to undergo
crushing in this world for his soul's sake. Had he not
wished to marry Linda himself, it might be very well
that Linda should marry a young man. But now that
Linda so openly scorned him, had treated him with such
plain-spoken contumely, he thought it would be well
that Linda should be crushed. Yes; and he thought also
that he might probably find a means of crushing her.

'I suppose, miss,' he said, after pausing for some moments, 'that the meaning of this is that you have got a
young lover?'

'I have got no young lover,' said Linda; 'and if I had,
why shouldn't I? What would that be to you?'

'It would be very much to me, if it be the young man
I think. Yes, I understand; you blush now. Very well.
I shall know now how to manage you;—or your aunt
will know.'

'I have got no lover,' said Linda, in great anger; 'and
you are a very wicked old man to say so.'

'Then you had better receive me as your future husband. If you will be good and obedient, I will forgive
the great unkindness of what you have said to me.'

'I have not meant to be unkind, but I cannot have
you for my husband. How am I to love you?'

'That will come.'

'It will never come.'

'Was it not unkind when you said that I was three times
as old as you?'

'I did not mean to be unkind.' Since the allusion
which had been made to some younger lover, from which
Linda had gathered that Peter Steinmarc must know
something of Ludovic's passion for herself, she had been
in part quelled. She was not able now to stand up
bravely before her suitor, and fight him as she had done
at first with all the weapons which she had at her command. The man knew something which it was almost
ruinous to her that he should know, something by which,

if her aunt knew it, she would be quite ruined. How could it be that Herr Steinmarc should have learned anything of Ludovic's wild love? He had not been in the house,—he had been in the town-hall, sitting in his big official arm-chair,—when Ludovic had stood in the low-arched doorway and blown a kiss across the river from his hand. And yet he did know it; and knowing it, would of course tell her aunt! 'I did not mean to be unkind,' she said.

'You were very unkind.'

'I beg your pardon then, Herr Steinmarc.'

'Will you let me address you, then, as your lover?'

'Oh, no!'

'Because of that young man; is it?'

'Oh, no, no. I have said nothing to the young man— not a word. He is nothing to me. It is not that.'

'Linda, I see it all. I understand everything now. Unless you will promise to give him up, and do as your aunt bids you, I must tell your aunt everything.'

'There is nothing to tell.'

'Linda!'

'I have done nothing. I can't help any young man. He is only over there because of the brewery.' She had told all her secret now. 'He is nothing to me, Herr Steinmarc, and if you choose to tell aunt Charlotte, you must. I shall tell aunt Charlotte that if she will let me keep out of your way, I will promise to keep out of his. But if you come, then—then—then—I don't know what I may do.' After that she escaped, and went away back into the kitchen, while Peter Steinmarc stumped up again to his own room.

'Well, my friend, how has it gone?' said Madam Staubach, entering Peter's chamber, at the door of which she had knocked.

'I have found out the truth,' said Peter, solemnly.

'What truth?' Peter shook his head, not despondently so much as in dismay. The thing which he had to tell was so very bad! He felt it so keenly, not on his own account so much as on account of his friend! All that was expressed by the manner in which Peter shook his head. 'What truth have you found out, Peter? Tell me at once,' said Madame Staubach.

'She has got a—lover.'

'Who? Linda! I do not believe it.'

'She has owned it. And such a lover!' Whereupon Peter Steinmarc lifted up both his hands.

'What lover? Who is he? How does she know him, and when has she seen him? I cannot believe it. Linda has never been false to me.'

'Her lover is—Ludovic Valcarm.'

'Your cousin?'

'My cousin Ludovic—who is a good-for-nothing, a spendthrift, a fellow without a florin, a fellow that plays cards on Sundays.'

'And who fears neither God nor Satan,' said Madame Staubach. 'Peter Steinmarc, I do not believe it. The child can hardly have spoken to him.'

'You had better ask her, Madame Staubach.' Then with some exaggeration Peter told Linda's aunt all that he did know, and something more than all that Linda had confessed; and before their conversation was over they had both agreed that, let these tidings be true in much or in little, or true not at all, every exertion should be used to force Linda into the proposed marriage with as little delay as possible.

'I overheard him speaking to her out of the street window, when they thought I was out,' said the town-clerk in a whisper before he left Madame Staubach. 'I had to come back home for the key of the big chest, and they never knew that I had been in the house.' This had been one of the occasions on which Linda had been addressed, and had wanted breath to answer the bold young man who had spoken to her.

CHAPTER IV

On the following morning, being Sunday morning, Linda positively refused to get up at the usual hour, and declared her intention of not going to church. She was, she said, so ill that she could not go to church. Late on the preceding evening Madame Staubach, after she had left Peter Steinmarc, had spoken to Linda of what she had heard, and it was not surprising that Linda should have a headache on the following morning. 'Linda,' Madame Staubach said, 'Peter has told me that Ludovic Valcarm has been—making love to you. Linda, is this true?' Linda had been unable to say that it was not true. Her aunt put the matter to her in a more cunning way than Steinmarc had done, and Linda felt herself unable to deny the charge. 'Then let me tell you, that of all the young women of whom I ever heard, you are the most deceitful,' continued Madame Staubach.

'Do not say that, aunt Charlotte; pray, do not say that.'

'But I do say it. Oh, that it should have come to this between you and me!'

'I have not deceived you. Indeed I have not. I don't want to see Ludovic again; never, if you do not wish it. I haven't said a word to him. Oh, aunt, pray believe me. I have never spoken a word to him;—in the way of what you mean.'

'Will you consent to marry Peter Steinmarc?' Linda hesitated a moment before she answered. 'Tell me, Miss; will you promise to take Peter Steinmarc as your husband?'

'I cannot promise that, aunt Charlotte.'

'Then I will never forgive you,—never. And God will never forgive you. I did not think it possible that my sister's child should have been so false to me.'

'I have not been false to you,' said Linda through her tears.

'And such a terrible young man, too; one who drinks, and gambles, and is a rebel; one of whom all the world speaks ill; a penniless spendthrift, to whom no decent girl would betroth herself. But, perhaps, you are to be his light-of-love!'

'It is a shame,—a great shame,—for you to say—such things,' said Linda, sobbing bitterly. 'No, I won't wait, I must go. I would sooner be dead than hear you say such things to me. So I would. I can't help it, if it's wicked. You make me say it.' Then Linda escaped from

the room, and went up to her bed; and on the next
morning she was too ill either to eat her breakfast or to
go to church.

Of course she saw nothing of Peter on that morning;
but she heard the creaking of his shoes as he went forth
after his morning meal, and I fear that her good wishes
for his Sunday work did not go with him on that Sabbath
morning. Three or four times her aunt was in her room,
but to her aunt Linda would say no more than that she
was sick and could not leave her bed. Madame Staubach
did not renew the revilings which she had poured forth
so freely on the preceding evening, partly influenced by
Linda's headache, and partly, perhaps, by a statement
which had been made to her by Tetchen as to the amount
of love-making which had taken place. 'Lord bless you,
ma'am, in any other house than this it would go for
nothing. Over at Jacob Heisse's, among his girls, it
wouldn't even have been counted at all,—such a few
words as that. Just the compliments of the day, and no
more.' Tetchen could not have heard it all, or she would
hardly have talked of the compliments of the day. When
Ludovic had told Linda that she was the fairest girl in all
Nuremberg, and that he never could be happy, not for an
hour, unless he might hope to call her his own, even
Tetchen, whose notions about young men were not over
strict, could not have taken such words as simply meaning the compliments of the day. But there was Linda
sick in bed, and this was Sunday morning, and nothing
further could be said or done on the instant. And, moreover, such love-making as had taken place did in truth
seem to have been perpetrated altogether on the side of
the young man. Therefore it was that Madame Staubach
spoke with a gentle voice as she prescribed to Linda some
pill or potion that might probably be of service, and then
went forth to her church.

Madame Staubach's prayers on a Sunday morning
were a long affair. She usually left the house a little after
ten, and did not return till past two. Soon after she was
gone, on the present occasion, Tetchen came up to Linda's room, and expressed her own desire to go to the

Frauenkirche,—for Tetchen was a Roman Catholic.
'That is, if you mean to get up, miss, I'll go,' said Tetchen.
Linda, turning in her bed, thought that her head would
be better now that her aunt was gone, and promised
that she would get up. In half an hour she was alone
in the kitchen down-stairs, and Tetchen had started to
the Frauenkirche,—or to whatever other place was more
agreeable to her for the occupation of her Sunday
morning.

It was by no means an uncommon occurrence that
Linda should be left alone in the house on some part of
the Sunday, and she would naturally have seated herself
with a book at the parlour window as soon as she had
completed what little there might be to be done in the
kitchen. But on this occasion there came upon her a
feeling of desolateness as she thought of her present condition. Not only was she alone now, but she must be
alone for ever. She had no friend left. Her aunt was
estranged from her. Peter Steinmarc was her bitterest
enemy. And she did not dare even to think of Ludovic
Valcarm. She had sauntered now into the parlour, and,
as she was telling herself that she did not dare to think
of the young man, she looked across the river, and there
he was standing on the water's edge.

She retreated back in the room,—so far back that it
was impossible that he should see her. She felt quite sure
that he had not seen her as yet, for his back had been
turned to her during the single moment that she had
stood at the window. What should she do now? She
was quite certain that he could not see her, as she stood
far back in the room, within the gloom of the dark walls.
And then there was the river between him and her. So
she stood and watched, as one might watch a coming
enemy, or a lover who was too bold. There was a little
punt or raft moored against the bank just opposite to
the gateway of the warehouse, which often lay there, and
which, as Linda knew, was used in the affairs of the
brewery. Now, as she stood watching him, Ludovic
stepped into the punt without unfastening it from the
ring, and pushed the loose end of it across the river as

far as the shallow bottom would allow him. But still
there was a considerable distance between him and the
garden of the red house, a distance so great that Linda
felt that the water made her safe. But there was a pole
in the boat, and Linda saw the young man take up the
pole and prepare for a spring, and in a moment he was
standing in the narrow garden. As he landed, he flung
the pole back into the punt, which remained stranded
in the middle of the river. Was ever such a leap seen
before? Then she thought how safe she would have been
from Peter Steinmarc, had Peter Steinmarc been in the
boat.

What would Ludovic Valcarm do next? He might
remain there all day before she would go to him. He
was now standing under the front of the centre gable,
and was out of Linda's sight. There was a low window
close to him where he stood, which opened from the
passage that ran through the middle of the house. On
the other side of this passage, opposite to the parlour
which Madame Staubach occupied, was a large room
not now used, and filled with lumber. Linda, as soon
as she was aware that Ludovic was in the island, within
a few feet of her, and that something must be done, retreated from the parlour back into the kitchen, and, as
she went, thoughtfully drew the bolt of the front door.
But she had not thought of the low window into the
passage, which in these summer days was always opened,
nor, if she had thought of it, could she have taken any
precaution in that direction. To have attempted to close
the window would have been to throw herself into the
young man's arms. But there was a bolt inside the
kitchen door, and that she drew. Then she stood in the
middle of the room listening. Had this been a thief who
had come when she was left in charge of the house, is it
thus she would have protected her own property and
her aunt's? It was no thief. But why should she run
from this man whom she knew,—whom she knew and
would have trusted had she been left to her own judgment of him? She was no coward. Were she to face the
man, she would fear no personal danger from him. He

would offer her no insult, and she thought that she could protect herself, even were he to insult her. It was not that that she feared,—but that her aunt should be able to say that she had received her lover in secret on this Sunday morning, when she had pretended that she was too ill to go to church!

She was all ears, and could hear that he was within the house. She had thought of the window the moment that she had barred the kitchen door, and knew that he would be within the house. She could hear him knock at the parlour door, and then enter the parlour. But he did not stay there a moment. Then she heard him at the foot of the stair, and with a low voice he called to her by her name. 'Linda, are you there?' But, of course, she did not answer him. It might be that he would fancy that she was not within the house and would retreat. He would hardly intrude into their bedrooms; but it might be that he would go as far as his cousin's apartments. 'Linda,' he said again,—'Linda, I know that you are in the house.' That wicked Tetchen! It could not be but that Tetchen had been a traitor. He went three or four steps up the stairs, and then, bethinking himself of the locality, came down again and knocked at once at the kitchen door. 'Linda,' he said, when he found that the door was barred,—'Linda, I know that you are here.'

'Go away,' said Linda. 'Why have you come here? You know that you should not be here.'

'Open the door for one moment, that you may listen to me. Open the door, and I will tell you all. I will go instantly when I have spoken to you, Linda; I will indeed.'

Then she opened the door. Why should she be a barred-up prisoner in her own house? What was there that she need fear? She had done nothing that was wrong, and would do nothing wrong. Of course, she would tell her aunt. If the man would force his way into the house, climbing in through an open window, how could she help it? If her aunt chose to misbelieve her, let it be so. There was need now that she should call upon herself for strength. All heaven and earth together should not make her marry Peter Steinmarc. Nor should earth and the evil one combined make her give herself to a young man after any fashion that should disgrace her mother's memory or her father's name. If her aunt doubted her, the sorrow would be great, but she must bear it. 'You have no right here,' she said as soon as she was confronted with the young man. 'You know that you should not be here. Go away.'

'Linda, I love you.'

'I don't want your love.'

'And now they tell me that my cousin Peter is to be your husband.'

'No, no. He will never be my husband.'

'You will promise that?'

'He will never be my husband.'

'Thanks, dearest; a thousand thanks for that. But your aunt is his friend. Is it not true?'

'Of course she is his friend.'

'And would give you to him?'

'I am not hers to give. I am not to be given away at all. I choose to stay as I am. You know that you are very wicked to be here; but I believe you want to get me into trouble.'

'Oh, Linda!'

'Then go. If you wish me to forgive you, go instantly.'

'Say that you love me, and I will be gone at once.'

'I will not say it.'

'And do you not love me,—a little? Oh, Linda, you are so dear to me!'

'Why do you not go? They tell me evil things of you, and now I believe them. If you were not very wicked you would not come upon me here, in this way, when I am alone, doing all that you possibly can to make me wretched.'

'I would give all the world to make you happy.'

'I have never believed what they said of you. I always thought that they were ill-natured and prejudiced, and that they spoke falsehoods. But now I shall believe them. Now I know that you are very wicked. You have no right to stand here. Why do you not go when I bid you?'

'But you forgive me?'

'Yes, if you go now,—at once.'

Then he seized her hand and kissed it. 'Dearest Linda, remember that I shall always love you; always be thinking of you; always hoping that you will some day love me a little. Now I am gone?'

'But which way?' said Linda—'you cannot jump back to the boat. The pole is gone. At the door they will see you from the windows.'

'Nobody shall see me. God bless you, Linda.' Then he again took her hand, though he did not, on this occasion, succeed in raising it as far as his lips. After that he ran down the passage, and, having glanced each way from the window, in half a minute was again in the garden. Linda, of course, hurried into the parlour, that she might watch him. In another half minute he was down over the little wall, into the river, and in three strides had gained the punt. The water, in truth, on that side was not much over his knees; but Linda thought he must be very wet. Then she looked round, to see if there were any eyes watching him. As far as she could see, there were no eyes.

Linda, when she was alone, was by no means contented with herself; and yet there was a sort of joy at her heart which she could not explain to herself, and of which, being keenly alive to it, she felt in great dread. What could be more wicked, more full of sin, than receiving, on a Sunday morning, a clandestine visit from a young man, and such a young man as Ludovic Valcarm? Her aunt had often spoken to her, with fear and trembling, of the mode of life in which their neighbours opposite lived. The daughters of Jacob Heisse were allowed to dance, and talk, and flirt, and, according to Madame Staubach, were living in fearful peril. For how much would such a man as Jacob Heisse, who thought of nothing but working hard, in order that his four girls might always have fine dresses,—for how much would he be called upon to answer in the last day? Of what comfort would it be to him then that his girls, in this foolish vain world, had hovered about him, bringing him his pipe and slippers, filling his glass stoup for him, and kissing his forehead as they stood over his easy-chair in the evening? Jacob Heisse and his daughters had ever been used as an example of worldly living by Madame Staubach. But none of Jacob Heisse's girls would ever have done such a thing as this. They flirted, indeed; but they did it openly, under their father's nose. And Linda had often heard the old man joke with his daughters about their lovers. Could Linda joke with any one touching this visit from Ludovic Valcarm?

And yet there was something in it that was a joy to her,—a joy which she could not define. Since her aunt had been so cruel to her, and since Peter had appeared before her as her suitor, she had told herself that she had no friend. Heretofore she had acknowledged Peter as her friend, in spite of his creaking shoes and objectionable hat. There was old custom in his favour, and he had not been unkind to her as an inmate of the same house with him. Her aunt she had loved dearly; but now her aunt's cruelty was so great that she shuddered as she thought of it. She had felt herself to be friendless. Then this young man had come to her; and though she had said to him all the hard things of which she could think because of his coming, yet—yet—yet she liked him because he had come. Was any other young man in Nuremberg so handsome? Would any other young man have taken that leap, or have gone through the river, that he might speak one word to her, even though he were to have nothing in return for the word so spoken? He had asked her to love him, and she had refused;—of course she had refused;—of course he had known that she would refuse. She would sooner have died than have told him that she loved him. But she thought she did love him— a little. She did not so love him but what she would give him up,—but what she would swear never to set eyes upon him again, if, as part of such an agreement, she might be set free from Peter Steinmarc's solicitations. That was a matter of course, because, without reference to Peter, she quite acknowledged that she was not free to have a lover of her own choice, without her aunt's consent. To give up Ludovic would be a duty,—a duty which she thought she could perform. But she would not perform it unless as part of a compact. No; let them look to it. If duty was expected from her, let duty be done to her. Then she sat thinking, and as she thought she kissed her own hand where Ludovic had kissed it.

The object of her thoughts was this;—what should she do now, when her aunt came home? Were she at once to tell her aunt all that had occurred, that comparison which she had made between herself and the Heisse girls, so much to her own disfavour, would not be a true comparison. In that case she would have received no clandestine young man. It could not be imputed to her as a fault,—at any rate not imputed by the justice of heaven, —that Ludovic Valcarm had jumped out of a boat and got in at the window. She could put herself right, at any rate, before any just tribunal, simply by telling the story truly and immediately. 'Aunt Charlotte, Ludovic Valcarm has been here. He jumped out of a boat, and got in at the window, and followed me into the kitchen, and kissed my hand, and swore he loved me, and then he scrambled back through the river. I couldn't help it;— and now you know all about it.' The telling of such a tale as that would, she thought, be the only way of making herself quite right before a just tribunal. But she felt, as she tried the telling of it to herself, that the task would be very difficult. And then her aunt would only half believe her, and would turn the facts, joined, as they would be, with her own unbelief, into additional grounds for urging on this marriage with Peter Steinmarc. How can one plead one's cause justly before a tribunal which is manifestly unjust,—which is determined to do injustice?

Moreover, was she not bound to secrecy? Had not secrecy been implied in that forgiveness which she had promised to Ludovic as the condition of his going? He had accepted the condition and gone. After that, would she not be treacherous to betray him? Why was it that at this moment it seemed to her that treachery to him,— to him who had treated her with such arrogant audacity,

—would be of all guilt the most guilty? It was true that she could not put herself right without telling of him; and not to put herself right in this extremity would be to fall into so deep a depth of wrong! But any injury to herself would now be better than treachery to him. Had he not risked much in order that he might speak to her that one word of love? But, for all that, she did not make up her mind for a time. She must be governed by things as they went.

Tetchen came home first, and to Tetchen, Linda was determined that she would say not a word. That Tetchen was in communication with young Valcarm she did not doubt, but she would not tell the servant what had been the result of her wickedness. When Tetchen came in, Linda was in the kitchen, but she went at once into the parlour, and there awaited her aunt. Tetchen had bustled in, in high good-humour, and had at once gone to work to prepare for the Sunday dinner. 'Mr. Peter is to dine with you to-day, Linda,' she had said; 'your aunt thinks there is nothing like making one family of it.' Linda had left the kitchen without speaking a word, but she had fully understood the importance of the domestic arrangement which Tetchen had announced. No stranger ever dined at her aunt's table; and certainly her aunt would have asked no guest to do so on a Sunday but one whom she intended to regard as a part of her own household. Peter Steinmarc was to be one of them, and therefore might be allowed to eat his dinner with them even on the Sabbath.

Between two and three her aunt came in, and Peter was with her. As was usual on Sundays, Madame Staubach was very weary, and, till the dinner was served, was unable to do much in the way of talking. Peter went up into his own room to put away his hat and umbrella, and then, if ever, would have been the moment for Linda to have told her story. But she did not tell it then. Her aunt was leaning back in her accustomed chair, with her eyes closed, as was often her wont, and Linda knew that her thoughts were far away, wandering in another world, of which she was ever thinking, living in a dream of bliss

with singing angels,—but not all happy, not all sure, because of the danger that must intervene. Linda could
not break in, at such a time as this, with her story of the
young man and his wild leap from the boat.

And certainly she would not tell her story before Peter
Steinmarc. It should go untold to her dying day before
she would whisper a word of it in his presence. When
they sat round the table, the aunt was very kind in her
manner to Linda. She had asked after her headache, as
though nothing doubting the fact of the ailment; and
when Linda had said that she had been able to rise almost
as soon as her aunt had left the house, Madame Staubach
expressed no displeasure. When the dinner was over,
Peter was allowed to light his pipe, and Madame Staubach either slept or appeared to sleep. Linda seated herself in the furthest corner of the room, and kept her eyes
fixed upon a book. Peter sat and smoked with his eyes
closed, and his great big shoes stuck out before him. In
this way they remained for an hour. Then Peter got up,
and expressed his intention of going out for a stroll in the
Nonnen Garten. Now the Nonnen Garten was close to
the house,—to be reached by a bridge across the river,
not fifty yards from Jacob Heisse's door. Would Linda
go with him? But Linda declined.

'You had better, my dear,' said Madame Staubach,
seeming to awake from her sleep. 'The air will do you
good.'

'Do, Linda,' said Peter; and then he intended to be
very gracious in what he added. 'I will not say a word
to tease you, but just take you out, and bring you back
again.'

'I am sure, it being the Sabbath, he would say nothing
of his hopes to-day,' said Madame Staubach.

'Not a word,' said Peter, lifting up one hand in token
of his positive assurance.

But, even so assured, Linda would not go with him,
and the town-clerk went off alone. Now, again, had
come the time in which Linda could tell the tale. It
must certainly be told now or never. Were she to tell it
now she could easily explain why she had been silent so

long; but were she not to tell it now, such explanation would ever afterwards be impossible. 'Linda, dear, will you read to me,' said her aunt. Then Linda took up the great Bible. 'Turn to the eighth and ninth chapters of Isaiah, my child.' Linda did as she was bidden, and read the two chapters indicated. After that, there was silence for a few minutes, and then the aunt spoke. 'Linda, my child.'

'Yes, aunt Charlotte.'

'I do not think you would willingly be false to me.' Then Linda turned away her face, and was silent. 'It is not that the offence to me would be great, who am, as we all are, a poor weak misguided creature; but that the sin against the Lord is so great, seeing that He has placed me here as your guide and protector.' Linda made no promise in answer to this, but even then she did not tell the tale. How could she have told it at such a moment? But the tale must now go untold for ever!

CHAPTER V

A WEEK passed by, and Linda Tressel heard nothing of Ludovic, and began at last to hope that that terrible episode of the young man's visit to her might be allowed to be as though it had never been. A week passed by, during every day of which Linda had feared and had half expected to hear some question from her aunt which would nearly crush her to the ground. But no such question had been asked, and, for aught that Linda knew, no one but she and Ludovic were aware of the wonderful jump that had been made out of the boat on to the island. And during this week little, almost nothing, was said to her in reference to the courtship of Peter Stein-marc. Peter himself spoke never a word; and Madame Staubach had merely said, in reference to certain pipes of tobacco which were smoked by the town-clerk in Madame Staubach's parlour, and which would heretofore have been smoked in the town-clerk's own room, that it was well that Peter should learn to make himself at home with them. Linda had said nothing in reply, but had sworn inwardly that she would never make herself at home with Peter Steinmarc.

In spite of the pipes of tobacco, Linda was beginning to hope that she might even yet escape from her double peril, and, perhaps, was beginning to have hope even beyond that, when she was suddenly shaken in her security by words which were spoken to her by Fanny Heisse. 'Linda,' said Fanny, running over to the gate of Madame Staubach's house, very early on one bright summer morning, 'Linda, it is to be to-morrow! And will you not come?'

'No, dear; we never go out here: we are so sad and solemn that we know nothing of gaiety.'

'You need not be solemn unless you like it.'

'I don't know but what I do like it, Fanny; I have become so used to it that I am as grave as an owl.'

'That comes of having an old lover, Linda.'

'I have not got an old lover,' said Linda, petulantly.

'You have got a young one, at any rate.'

'What do you mean, Fanny?'

'What do I mean? Just what I say. You know very well what I mean. Who was it jumped over the river that Sunday morning, my dear? I know all about it.' Then there came across Linda's face a look of extreme pain,—a look of anguish; and Fanny Heisse could see that her friend was greatly moved by what she had said. 'You don't suppose that I shall tell any one,' she added.

'I should not mind anything being told if all could be told,' said Linda.

'But he did come,—did he not?' Linda merely nodded her head. 'Yes; I knew that he came when your aunt was at church, and Tetchen was out, and Herr Steinmarc was out. Is it not a pity that he should be such a ne'er-do-well?'

'Do you think that I am a ne'er-do-well, Fanny?'

'No indeed; but, Linda, I will tell you what I have always thought about young men. They are very nice, and all that; and when old croaking hunkses have told me that I should have nothing to say to them, I have always answered that I meant to have as much to say to them as possible; but it is like eating good things;—everybody likes eating good things, but one feels ashamed of doing it in secret.'

This was a terrible blow to poor Linda. 'But I don't like doing it,' she answered. 'It wasn't my fault. I did not bid him come.'

'One never does bid them to come; I mean not till one has taken up with a fellow as a lover outright. Then you bid them, and sometimes they won't come for your bidding.'

'I would have given anything in the world to have prevented his doing what he did. I never mean to speak to him again,—if I can help it.'

'Oh, Linda!'

'I suppose you think I expected him, because I stayed at home alone?'

'Well,—I did think that possibly you expected something.'

'I would have gone to church with my aunt though my head was splitting had I thought that Herr Valcarm would have come here while she was away.'

'Mind I have not blamed you. It is a great shame to give a girl an old lover like Peter Steinmarc, and ask her to marry him. I wouldn't have married Peter Steinmarc for all the uncles and all the aunts in creation; nor yet for father,—though father would never have thought of such a thing. I think a girl should choose a lover for herself, though how she is to do so if she is to be kept moping at home always, I cannot tell. If I were treated as you are I think I should ask somebody to jump over the river to me.'

'I have asked nobody. But, Fanny, how did you know it?'

'A little bird saw him.'

'But, Fanny, do tell me.'

'Max saw him get across the river with his own eyes.' Max Bogen was the happy man who on the morrow was to make Fanny Heisse his wife.

'Heavens and earth!'

'But, Linda, you need not be afraid of Max. Of all men in the world he is the very last to tell tales.'

'Fanny, if ever you whisper a word of this to any one, I will never speak to you again.'

'Of course, I shall not whisper it.'

'I cannot explain to you all about it,—how it would ruin me. I think I should kill myself outright if my aunt were to know it; and yet I did nothing wrong. I would not encourage a man to come to me in that way for all the world; but I could not help his coming. I got myself into the kitchen; but when I found that he was in the house I thought it would be better to open the door and speak to him.'

'Very much better. I would have slapped his face. A lover should know when to come and when to stay away.'

'I was ashamed to think that I did not dare to speak to him, and so I opened the door. I was very angry with him.'

'But still, perhaps, you like him,—just a little; is not that true, Linda?'

'I do not know; but this I know, I do not want ever to see him again.'

'Come, Linda; never is a long time.'

'Let it be ever so long, what I say is true.'

'The worst of Ludovic is that he is a ne'er-do-well. He spends more money than he earns, and he is one of those wild spirits who are always making up some plan of politics—who live with one foot inside the State prison, as it were. I like a lover to be gay, and all that; but it is not well to have one's young man carried off and locked up by the burgomasters. But, Linda, do not be unhappy. Be sure that I shall not tell; and as for Max Bogen, his tongue is not his own. I should like to hear him say a word about such a thing when I tell him to be silent.'

Linda believed her friend, but still it was a great trouble to her that any one should know what Ludovic Valcarm had done on that Sunday morning. As she thought of it all, it seemed to her to be almost impossible that a secret should remain a secret that was known to three persons,—for she was sure that Tetchen knew it,—

to three persons besides those immediately concerned. She thought of her aunt's words to her, when Madame Staubach had cautioned her against deceit, 'I do not think that you would willingly be false to me, because the sin against the Lord would be so great.' Linda had understood well how much had been meant by this caution. Her aunt had groaned over her in spirit once, when she found it to be a fact that Ludovic Valcarm had been allowed to speak to her,—had been allowed to speak though it were but a dozen words. The dozen words had been spoken and had not been revealed, and Madame Staubach having heard of this sin, had groaned in the spirit heavily. How much deeper would be her groans if she should come to know that Ludovic had been received in her absence, had been received on a Sabbath morning, when her niece was feigning to be ill! Linda still fancied that her aunt might believe her if she were to tell her own story, but she was certain that her aunt would never believe her if the story were to be told by another. In that case there would be nothing for her, Linda, but perpetual war; and, as she thought, perpetual disgrace. As her aunt would in such circumstances range her forces on the side of propriety, so must she range hers on the side of impropriety. It would become necessary that she should surrender herself, as it were, to Satan; that she should make up her mind for an evil life; that she should cut altogether the cord which bound her to the rigid practices of her present mode of living. Her aunt had once asked her if she meant to be the light-of-love of this young man. Linda had well known what her aunt had meant, and had felt deep offence; but yet she now thought that she could foresee a state of things in which, though that degradation might yet be impossible, the infamy of such degradation would belong to her. She did not know how to protect herself from all this, unless she did so by telling her aunt of the young man's visit.

But were she to do so she must accompany her tale by the strongest assurance that no possible consideration would induce her to marry Peter Steinmarc. There must then be a compact, as has before been said, that the name neither of one man nor the other should ever again be mentioned as that of Linda's future husband. But would her aunt agree to such a compact? Would she not rather so use the story that would be told to her, as to draw from it additional reasons for pressing Peter's suit? The odious man still smoked his pipes of tobacco in Madame Staubach's parlour, gradually learning to make himself at home there. Linda, as she thought of this, became grave, settled, and almost ferocious in the working of her mind. Anything would be better than this,—even the degradation to be feared from hard tongues, and from the evil report of virtuous women. As she pictured to herself Peter Steinmarc with his big feet, and his straggling hairs, and his old hat, and his constant pipe, almost any lot in life seemed to her to be better than that. Any lot in death would certainly be better than that. No! If she told her story there must be a compact. And if her aunt would consent to no compact, then,—then she must give herself over to the Evil One. In that case there would be no possible friend for her, no ally available to her in her difficulties, but that one. In that case, even though Ludovic should have both feet within the State prison, he must be all in all to her, and she,—if possible,—all in all to him.

Then she was driven to ask herself some questions as to her feelings towards Ludovic Valcarm. Hitherto she had endeavoured to comfort herself with the reflection that she had in no degree committed herself. She had not even confessed to herself that she loved the man. She had never spoken,—she thought that she had never spoken a word, that could be taken by him as encouragement. But yet, as things were going with her now, she passed no waking hour without thinking of him; and in her sleeping hours he came to her in her dreams. Ah, how often he leaped over that river, beautifully, like an angel, and, running to her in her difficulties, dispersed all her troubles by the beauty of his presence. But then the scene would change, and he would become a fiend instead of a god, or a fallen angel; and at these moments it would become her fate to be carried off with him into uttermost darkness. But even in her saddest dreams she was never inclined to stand before the table in the church and vow that she would be the loving wife of Peter Steinmarc. Whenever in her dreams such a vow was made, the promise was always given to that ne'er-do-well.

Of course she loved the man. She came to know it as a fact, to be quite sure that she loved him, without reaching any moment in which she first made the confession openly to herself. She knew that she loved him. Had she not loved him, would she have so easily forgiven him,— so easily have told him that he was forgiven? Had she not loved him, would not her aunt have heard the whole story from her on that Sunday evening, even though the two chapters of Isaiah had been left unread in order that she might tell it? Perhaps, after all, the compact of which she had been thinking might be more difficult to her than she had imagined. If the story of Ludovic's coming could be kept from her aunt's ears, it might even yet be possible to her to keep Steinmarc at a distance without any compact. One thing was certain to her. He should be kept at a distance, either with or without a compact.

Days went on, and Fanny Heisse was married, and all probability of telling the story was at an end. Madame Staubach had asked her niece why she did not go to her friend's wedding, but Linda had made no answer,—had shaken her head as though in anger. What business had her aunt to ask her why she did not make one of a gay assemblage, while everything was being done to banish all feeling of gaiety from her life? How could there be any pleasant thought in her mind while Peter Steinmarc still smoked his pipes in their front parlour? Her aunt understood this, and did not press the question of the wedding party. But, after so long an interval, she did find it necessary to press that other question of Peter's courtship. It was now nearly a month since the matter had first been opened to Linda, and Madame Staubach was resolved that the thing should be settled before the autumn was over. 'Linda,' she said one day, 'has Peter Steinmarc spoken to you lately?'

'Has he spoken to me, aunt Charlotte?'

'You know what I mean, Linda.'

'No, he has not—spoken to me. I do not mean that he should—speak to me.' Linda, as she made this answer, put on a hard stubborn look, such as her aunt did not know that she had ever before seen upon her countenance. But if Linda was resolved, so also was Madame Staubach.

'My dear,' said the aunt, 'I do not know what to think of such an answer. Herr Steinmarc has a right to speak if he pleases, and certainly so when that which he says is said with my full concurrence.'

'I can't allow you to think that I shall ever be his wife. That is all.'

After this there was silence for some minutes, and then Madame Staubach spoke again. 'My dear, have you thought at all about—marriage?'

'Not much, aunt Charlotte.'

'I daresay not, Linda; and yet it is a subject on which a young woman should think much before she either accepts or rejects a proposed husband.'

'It is enough to know that one doesn't like a man.'

'No, that is not enough. You should examine the causes of your dislike. And as far as mere dislike goes, you should get over it, if it be unjust. You ought to do that, whoever may be the person in question.'

'But it is not mere dislike.'

'What do you mean, Linda?'

'It is disgust.'

'Linda, that is very wicked. You should not allow yourself to feel what you call disgust at any of God's creatures. Have you ever thought who made Herr Steinmarc?'

'God made Judas Iscariot, aunt Charlotte.'

'Linda, that is profane,—very profane.' Then there was silence between them again; and Linda would have remained silent had her aunt permitted it. She had been called profane, but she disregarded that, having, as she thought, got the better of her aunt in the argument as to disgust felt for any of God's creatures. But Madame

Staubach had still much to say. 'I was asking you whether you had thought at all about marriage, and you told me that you had not.'

'I have thought that I could not possibly—under any circumstances—marry Peter Steinmarc.'

'Linda, will you let me speak? Marriage is a very solemn thing.'

'Very solemn indeed, aunt Charlotte.'

'In the first place, it is the manner in which the all-wise Creator has thought fit to make the weaker vessel subject to the stronger one.' Linda said nothing, but thought that that old town-clerk was not a vessel strong enough to hold her in subjection. 'It is this which a woman should bring home to herself, Linda, when she first thinks of marriage.'

'Of course I should think of it, if I were going to be married.'

'Young women too often allow themselves to imagine that wedlock should mean pleasure and diversion. Instead of that it is simply the entering into that state of life in which a woman can best do her duty here below. All life here must be painful, full of toil, and moistened with many tears.' Linda was partly prepared to acknowledge the truth of this teaching; but she thought that there was a great difference in the bitterness of tears. Were she to marry Ludovic Valcarm, her tears with him would doubtless be very bitter, but no tears could be so bitter as those which she would be called upon to shed as the wife of Peter Steinmarc. 'Of course,' continued Madame Staubach, 'a wife should love her husband.'

'But I could not love Peter Steinmarc.'

'Will you listen to me? How can you understand me if you will not listen to me? A wife should love her husband. But young women, such as I see them to be, because they have been so instructed, want to have something soft and delicate; a creature without a single serious thought, who is chosen because his cheek is red and his hair is soft; because he can dance, and speak vain, meaningless words; because he makes love, as the foolish parlance of the world goes. And we see what comes of such lovemaking. Oh, Linda! God forbid that you should fall into that snare! If you will think of it, what is it but harlotry?'

'Aunt Charlotte, do not say such horrible things.'

'A woman when she becomes a man's wife should see, above all things, that she is not tempted by the devil after this fashion. Remember, Linda, how he goeth about,— ever after our souls,—like a roaring lion. And it is in this way specially that he goeth about after the souls of young women.'

'But why do you say those things to me?'

'It is to you only that I can say them. I would so speak to all young women, if it were given me to speak to more than to one. You talk of love.'

'No, aunt; never. I do not talk—of love.'

'Young women do, and think of it, not knowing what love for their husband should mean. A woman should revere her husband and obey him, and be subject to him in everything.' Was it supposed, Linda thought, that she should revere such a being as Peter Steinmarc? What could be her aunt's idea of reverence? 'If she does that, she will love him also.'

'Yes,—if she does,' said Linda.

'And will not this be much more likely, if the husband be older than his wife?'

'A year or two,' said Linda, timidly.

'Not a year or two only, but so much so as to make him graver and wiser, and fit to be in command over her. Will not the woman so ruled be safer than she who trusts herself with one who is perhaps as weak and inexperienced as herself?' Madame Staubach paused, but Linda would not answer the question. She did not wish for such security as was here proposed to her. 'Is it not that of which you have to think,—your safety here, so that, if possible, you may be safe hereafter?' Linda answered this to herself, within her own bosom. Not for security here or hereafter, even were such to be found by such means, would she consent to become the wife of the man proposed to her. Madame Staubach, finding that no spoken reply was given to her questions, at last proceeded from generalities to the special case which she had under her consideration. 'Linda,' she said, 'I trust you will consent to become the wife of this excellent man.' Linda's face became very hard, but still she said nothing. 'The danger of which I have spoken is close upon you. You must feel it to be so. A youth, perhaps the most notorious in all Nuremberg for wickedness——'

'No, aunt; no.'

'I say yes; and this youth is spoken of openly as your lover.'

'No one has a right to say so.'

'It is said, and he has so addressed himself to your own ears. You have confessed it. Tell me that you will do as I would have you, and then I shall know that you are safe. Then I will trust you in everything, for I shall be sure that it will be well with you. Linda, shall it be so?'

'It shall not be so, aunt Charlotte.'

'Is it thus you answer me?'

'Nothing shall make me marry a man whom I hate.'

'Hate him! Oh, Linda.'

'Nothing shall make me marry a man whom I cannot love.'

'You fancy, then, that you love that reprobate?' Linda was silent. 'Is it so? Tell me. I have a right to demand an answer to that question.'

'I do love him,' said Linda. Using the moment for reflection allowed to her as best she could, she thought that she saw the best means of escape in this avowal. Surely her aunt would not press her to marry one man when she had declared that she loved another.

'Then, indeed, you are a castaway.'

'I am no castaway, aunt Charlotte,' said Linda, rising to her feet. 'Nor will I remain here, even with you, to be so called. I have done nothing to deserve it. If you will cease to press upon me this odious scheme, I will do nothing to disgrace either myself or you; but if I am perplexed by Herr Steinmarc and his suit, I will not answer for the consequences.' Then she turned her back upon her aunt and walked slowly out of the room.

On that very evening Peter came to Linda while she

was standing alone at the kitchen window. Tetchen was
out of the house, and Linda had escaped from the parlour
as soon as the hour arrived at which in those days Steinmarc was wont to seat himself in her aunt's presence
and slowly light his huge meerschaum pipe. But on this
occasion he followed her into the kitchen, and Linda was
aware that this was done before her aunt had had any
opportunity of explaining to him what had occurred on
that morning. 'Fraulein,' he said, 'as you are alone here,
I have ventured to come in and join you.'

'This is no proper place for you, Herr Steinmarc,' she
replied. Now, it was certainly the case that Peter rarely
passed a day without standing for some twenty minutes
before the kitchen stove talking to Tetchen. Here he
would always take off his boots when they were wet, and
here, on more than one occasion,—on more, probably,
than fifty,—had he sat and smoked his pipe, when there
was no other stove a-light in the house to comfort him
with its warmth. Linda, therefore, had no strong point
in her favour when she pointed out to her suitor that he
was wrong to intrude upon the kitchen.

'Wherever you are, must be good for me,' said Peter,
trying to smirk and to look pleased.

Linda was determined to silence him, even if she could
not silence her aunt. 'Herr Steinmarc,' she said, 'I have
explained to my aunt that this kind of thing from you
must cease. It must be made to cease. If you are a man
you will not persecute me by a proposal which I have
told you already is altogether out of the question. If
there were not another man in all Nuremberg, I would
not have you. You may perhaps make me hate you
worse than anybody in the world; but you cannot possibly do anything else. Go to my aunt and you will find
that I have told her the same.' Then she walked off to
her own bedroom, leaving the town-clerk in sole possession of the kitchen.

Peter Steinmarc, when he was left standing alone in
the kitchen, did not like his position. He was a man not
endowed with much persuasive gift of words, but he had
a certain strength of his own. He had a will, and some

firmness in pursuing the thing which he desired. He was industrious, patient, and honest with a sort of second-class honesty. He liked to earn what he took, though he had a strong bias towards believing that he had earned whatever in any way he might have taken, and after the same fashion he was true with a second-class truth. He was unwilling to deceive; but he was usually able to make himself believe that that which would have been deceit from another to him, was not deceit from him to another. He was friendly in his nature to a certain degree, understanding that good offices to him-wards could not be expected unless he also was prepared to do good offices to others; but on this matter he kept an accurate mental account-sheet, on which he strove hard to be able to write the balance always on the right side. He was not cruel by nature, but he had no tenderness of heart and no delicacy of perception. He could forgive an offence against his comfort, as when Tetchen would burn his soup; or even against his pocket, as when, after many struggles, he would be unable to enforce the payment of some municipal fee. But he was vain, and could not forgive an offence against his person. Linda had previously told him to his face that he was old, and had with premeditated malice and falsehood exaggerated his age. Now she threatened him with her hatred. If he persevered in asking her to be his wife, she would hate him! He, too, began to hate her; but his hatred was unconscious, a thing of which he was himself unaware, and he still purposed that she should be his wife. He would break her spirit, and bring her to his feet, and punish her with a life-long punishment for saying that he was sixty, when, as she well knew, he was only fifty-two. She should beg for his love,—she who had threatened him with her hatred! And if she held out against him, he would lead her such a life, by means of tales told to Madame Staubach, that she should gladly accept any change as a release. He never thought of the misery that might be forthcoming to himself in the possession of a young wife procured after such a fashion. A man requires some power of imagination to enable him to look forward to the

circumstances of an untried existence, and Peter Steinmarc was not an imaginative man.

But he was a thoughtful man, cunning withal, and
conscious that various resources might be necessary to
him. There was a certain packer of casks, named Stobe,
in the employment of the brewers who owned the warehouse opposite, and Stobe was often to be seen on the
other side of the river in the Ruden Platz. With this man
Steinmarc had made an acquaintance, not at first with
any reference to Linda Tressel, but because he was
desirous of having some private information as to the
doings of his relative Ludovic Valcarm. From Stobe,
however, he had received the first intimation of Ludovic's
passion for Linda; and now on this very evening of which
we are speaking, he obtained further information,—
which shocked him, frightened him, pained him exceedingly, and yet gave him keen gratification. Stobe also
had seen the leap out of the boat, and the rush through
the river; and when, late on that evening, Peter Steinmarc, sore with the rebuff which he had received from
Linda, pottered over to the Ruden Platz, thinking that it
would be well that he should be very cunning, that he
should have a spy with his eye always open, that he
should learn everything that could be learned by one who
might watch the red house, and watch Ludovic also, he
learned, all of a sudden, by the speech of a moment, that
Ludovic Valcarm had, on that Sunday morning, paid
his wonderful visit to the island.

'So you mean that you saw him?' said Peter.

'With my own eyes,' said Stobe, who had his reasons,
beyond Peter's moderate bribes, for wishing to do an evil
turn to Ludovic. 'And I saw her at the parlour window,
watching him, when he came back through the water.'

'How long was he with her?' asked Peter, groaning,
but yet exultant.

'A matter of half an hour; not less anyways.'

'It was two Sundays since', said Peter, remembering
well the morning on which Linda had declined to go to
church because of her headache.

'I remember it well. It was the feast of St. Lawrence,'

said Stobe, who was a Roman Catholic, and mindful of the festivals of his Church.

Peter tarried for no further discourse with the brewer's man, but hurried back again, round by the bridge, to the red house. As he went he applied his mind firmly to the task of resolving what he would do. He might probably take the most severe revenge on Linda, the revenge which should for the moment be the most severe, by summoning her to the presence of her aunt, by there exposing her vile iniquity, and by there declaring that it was out of the question that a man so respectable as he should contaminate himself by marrying so vile a creature. But were he to do this Linda would never be in his power, and the red house would never be in his possession. Moreover, though he continued to tell himself that Linda was vile, though he was prepared to swear to her villany, he did not in truth believe that she had done anything disgraceful. That she had seen her lover he did not doubt; but that, in Peter's own estimation, was a thing to be expected. He must, no doubt, on this occasion pretend to view the matter with the eyes of Madame Staubach. In punishing Linda, he would so view it. But he thought that, upon the whole bearing of the case, it would not be incumbent upon his dignity to abandon for ever his bride and his bride's property, because she had been indiscreet. He would marry her still. But before he did so he would let her know how thoroughly she was in his power, and how much she would owe to him if he now took her to his bosom. The point on which he could not at once quite make up his mind was this: Should he tell Madame Staubach first, or should he endeavour to use the power over Linda, which his knowledge gave him, by threats to her? Might he not say to her with much strength, 'Give way to me at once, or I will reveal to your aunt this story of your vileness'? This no doubt would be the best course, could he trust in its success. But, should it not succeed, he would then have injured his position. He was afraid that Linda would be too high-spirited, too obstinate, and he resolved that his safest course would be to tell everything at once to Madame Staubach.

As he passed between the back of Jacob Heisse's house and the river he saw the upholsterer's ruddy face looking out from an open window belonging to his workshop. 'Good evening, Peter,' said Jacob Heisse. 'I hope the ladies are well.'

'Pretty well, I thank you,' said Peter, as he was hurrying by.

'Tell Linda that we take it amiss that she did not come to our girl's wedding. The truth is, Peter, you keep her too much moped up there among you. You should remember, Peter, that too much work makes Jack a dull boy. Linda will give you all the slip some day, if she be kept so tight in hand.'

Peter muttered something as he passed on to the red house. Linda would give them the slip, would she? It was not improbable, he thought, that she should try to do so, but he would keep such a watch on her that it should be very difficult, and the widow should watch as closely as he would do. Give them the slip! Yes; that might be possible, and therefore he would lose no time.

When he entered the house he walked at once up to Madame Staubach's parlour, and entered it without any of that ceremony of knocking that was usual to him. It was not that he intended to put all ceremony aside, but that in his eager haste he forgot his usual precaution. When he entered the room Linda was there with her aunt, and he had again to turn the whole subject over in his thoughts. Should he tell his tale in Linda's presence or behind her back? It gradually became apparent to him that he could not possibly tell it before her face; but he did not arrive at this conclusion without delay, and the minutes which were so occupied were full of agony. He seated himself in his accustomed chair, and looked from the aunt to the niece and then from the niece to the aunt. Give him the slip, would she? Well, perhaps she would. But she should be very clever if she did.

'I thought you would have been in earlier, Peter,' said Madame Staubach.

'I was coming, but I saw the fraulein in the kitchen,

and I ventured to speak a word or two there. The reception which I received drove me away.'

'Linda, what is this?'

'I did not think, aunt, that the kitchen was the proper place for him.'

'Any room in this house is the proper place for him,' said Madame Staubach, in her enthusiasm. Linda was silent, and Peter replied to this expression of hospitality simply by a grateful nod. 'I will not have you give yourself airs, Linda,' continued Madame Staubach. 'The kitchen not a proper place! What harm could Peter do in the kitchen?'

'He tormented me, so I left him. When he torments me I shall always leave him.' Then Linda got up and stalked out of the room. Her aunt called her more than once, but she would not return. Her life was becoming so heavy to her, that it was impossible that she should continue to endure it. She went up now to her room, and looking out of the window fixed her eyes upon the low stone archway in which she had more than once seen Ludovic Valcarm. But he was not there now. She knew, indeed, that he was not in Nuremberg. Tetchen had told her that he had gone to Augsburg,—on pretence of business connected with the brewery, Tetchen had said, but in truth with reference to some diabolical political scheme as to which Tetchen expressed a strong opinion that all who dabbled in it were children of the very devil. But though Ludovic was not in Nuremberg, Linda stood looking at the archway for more than half an hour, considering the circumstances of her life, and planning, if it might be possible to plan, some future scheme of existence. To live under the upas-tree of Peter Steinmarc's courtship would be impossible to her. But how should she avoid it? As she thought of this, her eyes were continually fixed on the low archway. Why did not he come out from it and give her some counsel as to the future? There she stood looking out of the window till she was called by her aunt's voice—'Linda, Linda, come down to me.' Her aunt's voice was very solemn, almost as though it came from the grave; but then solemnity was common to her aunt, and Linda, as she descended, had not on her mind any special fear.

When she reached the parlour Madame Staubach was alone there, standing in the middle of the room. For a moment or two after she entered, the widow stood there without speaking, and then Linda knew that there was cause for fear. 'Did you want me, aunt Charlotte?' she said.

'Linda, what were you doing on the morning of the Sabbath before the last, when I went to church alone, leaving you in bed?'

Linda was well aware now that her aunt knew it all, and was aware also that Steinmarc had been the informer. No idea of denying the truth of the story or of concealing anything, crossed her mind for a moment. She was quite prepared to tell everything now, feeling no doubt but that everything had been told. There was no longer a hope that she should recover her aunt's affectionate good-will. But in what words was she to tell her tale? That was now her immediate difficulty. Her aunt was standing before her, hard, stern, and cruel, expecting an answer to her question. How was that answer to be made on the spur of the moment?

'I did nothing, aunt Charlotte. A man came here while you were absent.'

'What man?'

'Ludovic Valcarm.' They were both standing, each looking the other full in the face. On Madame Staubach's countenance there was written a degree of indignation and angry shame which seemed to threaten utter repudiation of her niece. On Linda's was written a resolution to bear it all without flinching. She had no hope now with her aunt,—no other hope than that of being able to endure. For some moments neither of them spoke, and then Linda, finding it difficult to support her aunt's continued gaze, commenced her defence. 'The young man came when I was alone, and made his way into the house when the door was bolted. I had locked myself into the kitchen; but when I heard his voice I opened the door, thinking that it did not become me to be afraid of his presence.'

'Why did you not tell me,—at once?' Linda made no immediate reply to this question; but when Madame Staubach repeated it, she was obliged to answer.

'I told him that if he would go, I would forgive him. Then he went, and I thought that I was bound by my promise to be silent.'

Madame Staubach having heard this, turned round slowly, and walked to the window, leaving Linda in the middle of the room. There she stood for perhaps half a minute, and then came slowly back again. Linda had remained where she was, without stirring a limb; but her mind had been active, and she had determined that she would submit in silence to no rebukes. Any commands from her aunt, save one, she would endeavour to obey; but from all accusations as to impropriety of conduct she would defend herself with unabashed spirit. Her aunt came up close to her; and, putting out one hand, with the palm turned towards her, raising it as high as her shoulder, seemed to wave her away. 'Linda,' said Madame Staubach, 'you are a castaway.'

'I am no castaway, aunt Charlotte,' said Linda, almost jumping from her feet, and screaming in her self-defence.

'You will not frighten me by your wicked violence. You have—lied to me;—have lied to me. Yes; and that after all that I said to you as to the heinousness of such wickedness. Linda, it is my belief that you knew that he was coming when you kept your bed on that Sabbath morning.'

'If you choose to have such thoughts of me in your heart, aunt Charlotte, I cannot help it. I knew nothing of his coming. I would have given all I had to prevent it. Yes,—though his coming could do me no real harm. My good name is more precious to me than anything short of my self-esteem. Nothing even that you can say shall rob me of that.'

Madame Staubach was almost shaken by the girl's firmness,—by that, and by her own true affection for the sinner. In her bosom, what remained of the softness of womanhood was struggling with the hardness of the religious martinet, and with the wilfulness of the domestic tyrant. She had promised to Steinmarc that she would be very stern. Steinmarc had pointed out to her that nothing but the hardest severity could be of avail. He, in telling his story, had taken it for granted that Linda had expected her lover, had remained at home on purpose that she might receive her lover, and had lived a life of deceit with her aunt for months past. When Madame Staubach had suggested that the young man's coming might have been accidental, he had treated the idea with ridicule. He, as the girl's injured suitor, was, he declared, obliged to treat such a suggestion as altogether incredible, although he was willing to pardon the injury done to him, if a course of intense severity and discipline were at once adopted, and if this were followed by repentance which to him should appear to be sincere. When he took this high ground, as a man having authority, and as one who knew the world, he had carried Madame Staubach with him, and she had not ventured to say a word in excuse for her niece. She had promised that the severity should be at any rate forthcoming, and, if possible, the discipline. As for the repentance, that, she said meekly, must be left in the hands of God. 'Ah!' said Peter, in his bitterness, 'I would make her repent in sackcloth and ashes!' Then Madame Staubach had again promised that the sackcloth and ashes should be there. She remembered all this as she thought of relenting,—as she perceived that to relent would be sweet to her, and she made herself rigid with fresh resolves. If the man's coming had been accidental, why had not the story been told to her? She could understand nothing of that forgiveness of which Linda had spoken; and had not Linda confessed that she loved this man? Would she not rather have hated him who had so intruded upon her, had there been real intrusion in the visit?

'You have done that,' she said, 'which would destroy the character of any girl in Nuremberg.'

'If you mean, aunt Charlotte, that the thing which has happened would destroy the character of any girl in Nuremberg, it may perhaps be true. If so, I am very unfortunate.'

'Have you not told me that you love him?'

'I do;—I do;—I do! One cannot help one's love. To love as I do is another misfortune. There is nothing but misery around me. You have heard the whole truth now, and you may as well spare me further rebuke.'

'Do you not know how such misery should be met?' Linda shook her head. 'Have you prayed to be forgiven this terrible sin?'

'What sin?' said Linda, again almost screaming in her energy.

'The terrible sin of receiving this man in the absence of your friends.'

'It was no sin. I am sinful, I know,—very; no one perhaps more so. But there was no sin there. Could I help his coming? Aunt Charlotte, if you do not believe me about this, it is better that we should never speak to each again. If so, we must live apart.'

'How can that be? We cannot rid ourselves of each other.'

'I will go anywhere,—into service, away from Nuremberg,—where you will. But I will not be told that I am a liar.'

And yet Madame Staubach was sure that Linda had lied. She thought that she was sure. And if so,—if it were the case that this young woman had planned an infamous scheme for receiving her lover on a Sunday morning;—the fact that it was on a Sunday morning, and that the hour of the Church service had been used, greatly enhanced the atrocity of the sin in the estimation of Madame Staubach;—if the young woman had intrigued in order that her lover might come to her, of course she would intrigue again. In spite of Linda's solemn protestation as to her self-esteem, the thing would be going on. This infamous young man, who, in Madame Staubach's eyes, was beginning to take the proportions of the Evil One himself, would be coming there beneath her very nose. It seemed to her that life would be impossible to her, unless Linda would consent to be married to the respectable suitor who was still willing to receive her; and that the only way in which to exact that consent would be to insist on the degradation to which Linda had subjected herself. Linda had talked of going into service. Let her go into that service which was now offered to her by those whom she was bound to obey. 'Of course Herr Steinmarc knows it all,' said Madame Staubach.

'I do not regard in the least what Herr Steinmarc knows,' replied Linda.

'But he is still willing to overlook the impropriety of your conduct, upon condition——'

'He overlook it! Let him dare to say such a word to me, and I would tell him that his opinion in this matter was of less moment to me than that of any other creature in all Nuremberg. What is it to him who comes to me? Were it but for him, I would bid the young man come every day.'

'Linda!'

'Do not talk to me about Peter Steinmarc, aunt Charlotte, or I shall go mad.'

'I must talk about him, and you must hear about him. It is now more than ever necessary that you should be his wife. All Nuremberg will hear of this.'

'Of course it will,—as Peter Steinmarc knows it.'

'And how will you cover yourself from your shame?'

'I will not cover myself at all. If you are ashamed of me, I will go away. If you will not say that you are not ashamed of me, I will go away. I have done nothing to disgrace me, and I will hear nothing about shame.' Having made this brave assertion, she burst into tears, and then escaped to her own bed.

When Madame Staubach was left alone, she sat down, closed her eyes, clasped her hands, and began to pray. As to what she should do in these terrible circumstances she had no light, unless such light might be given to her from above. A certain trust she had in Peter Steinmarc, because Peter was a man, and not a young man; but it was not a trust which made her confident. She thought that Peter was very good in being willing to take Linda at all after all that had happened, but she had begun to be aware that he himself was not able to make his own goodness apparent to Linda. She did not in her heart blame Peter for his want of eloquence, but rather imputed an increased degree of culpability to Linda, in that any eloquence was necessary for her conviction on such a matter. Eloquence in an affair of marriage, in reference to any preparation for marriage arrangements, was one of those devil's baits of which Madame Staubach was especially afraid. Ludovic Valcarm no doubt could be eloquent, could talk of love, and throw glances from his eyes, and sigh, and do worse things, perhaps, even than those. All tricks of Satan, these to ensnare the souls of young women! Peter could perform no such tricks, and therefore it was that his task was so difficult to him. She could not regard it as a deficiency that he was unable to do those very things which, when done in her presence, were abominable to her sight, and when spoken of were abominable to her ears, and when thought of were abominable to her imagination. But yet how was she to arrange this marriage, if Peter were able to say nothing for himself? So she sat herself down and clasped her hands and prayed earnestly that assistance might be given to her. If you pray that a mountain shall be moved, and will have faith, the mountain shall certainly be stirred. So she told herself; but she told herself this in an agony of spirit, because she still doubted,—she feared that she doubted,—that this thing would not be done for her by heaven's aid. Oh, if she could only make herself certain that heaven would aid her, then the thing would be done for her. She could not be certain, and therefore she felt herself to be a wretched sinner.

In the mean time, Linda was in bed up-stairs, thinking over her position, and making up her mind as to what should be her future conduct. As far as it might be possible, she would enter no room in which Peter Steinmarc was present. She would not go into the parlour when he was there, even though her aunt should call her. Should he follow her into the kitchen, she would instantly leave it. On no pretence would she speak to him. She had always the refuge of her own bedroom, and should he venture to follow her there, she thought that she would know how to defend herself. As to the rest, she must bear

her aunt's thoughts, and if necessary her aunt's hard
words also. It was very well to talk of going into service,
but where was the house that would receive her? And
then, as to Ludovic Valcarm! In regard to him, it was
not easy for her to come to any resolution; but she still
thought that she would be willing to make that compact,
if her aunt, on the other side, would be willing to make it
also.

CHAPTER VI

ALL September went by, and all October, and life in
the red house in the island in Nuremberg was a very
sad life indeed. During this time Linda Tressel never
spoke to Ludovic Valcarm, nor of him; but she saw him
once, standing among the beer-casks opposite to the
warehouse. Had she not so seen him, she would have
thought that he had vanished altogether out of the city,
and that he was to be no more heard of or seen among
them. He was such a man, and belonged to such a set,
that his vanishing in this fashion would have been a thing
to create no surprise. He might have joined his father,
and they two might be together in any quarter of the
globe,—on any spot,—the more distant, the more probable. It was one of Linda's troubles that she knew
really nothing of the life of the man she loved. She had
always heard things evil spoken of him, but such evil-
speaking had come from those who were his enemies,—
from his cousin, who had been angry because Ludovic
had not remained with him on the stool in the town-hall;
and from Madame Staubach, who thought ill of almost
all young men, and who had been specially prejudiced
against this young man by Peter Steinmarc. Linda did
not know what she should believe. She had heard that
the Brothers Sach were respectable tradesmen, and it was
in Valcarm's favour that he was employed by them.
She had thought that he had left them; but now, seeing
him again among the barrels, she had reason to presume
that his life could not be altogether unworthy of him. He
was working for his bread, and what more could be

required from a young man than that? Nevertheless, when she saw him, she sedulously kept herself from his sight, and went, almost at once, back to the kitchen, from whence there was no view on to the Ruden Platz.

During these weeks life was very sad in this house. Madame Staubach said but little to her niece of her past iniquity in the matter of Ludovic's visit, and not much of Peter's suit; but she so bore herself that every glance of her eye, every tone of her voice, every nod of her head, was a separate rebuke. She hardly ever left Linda alone, requiring her company when she went out to make her little purchases in the market, and always on those more momentous and prolonged occasions when she attended some public prayer-meeting. Linda resolved to obey in such matters, and she did obey. She went hither and thither by her aunt's side, and at home sat with her aunt, always with a needle in her hand,—never leaving the room, except when Peter Steinmarc entered it. This he did, perhaps, on every other evening; and when he did so, Linda always arose and went up to her own chamber, speaking no word to the man as she passed him. When her aunt had rebuked her for this, laying upon her a command that she should remain when Steinmarc appeared, she protested that in that matter obedience was impossible to her. In all other things she would do as she was bidden; nothing, she said, but force, should induce her to stay for five minutes in the same room with Peter Steinmarc. Peter, who was of course aware of all this, would look at her when he passed her, or met her on the stairs, or in the passages, as though she were something too vile for him to touch. Madame Staubach, as she saw this, would groan aloud, and then Peter would groan. Latterly, too, Tetchen had taken to groaning; so that life in that house had become very sad. But Linda paid back Peter's scorn with interest. Her lips would curl, and her nostrils would be dilated, and her eyes would flash fire on him as she passed him. He also prayed a little in these days that Linda might be given into his hands. If ever she should be so given, he should teach her what it was to scorn the offer of an honest man.

For a month or six weeks Linda Tressel bore all this with patience; but when October was half gone, her patience was almost at an end. Such a life, if prolonged much further, would make her mad. The absence of all smiles from the faces of those with whom she lived, was terrible to her. She was surrounded by a solemnity as of the grave, and came to doubt almost whether she were a living creature. If she were to be scorned always, to be treated ever as one unfit for the pleasant intercourse of life, it might be as well that she should deserve such treatment. It was possible that by deserving it she might avoid it! At first, during these solemn wearisome weeks, she would tell herself that because her aunt had condemned her, not therefore need she feel assured that she was condemned of her heavenly Father. She was not a castaway because her aunt had so called her. But gradually there came upon her a feeling, springing from her imagination rather than from her judgment, that she was a thing set apart as vile and bad. There grew upon her a conviction that she was one of the non-elect, or rather, one of those who are elected to an eternity of misery. Her religious observances, as they came to her now, were odious to her; and that she supposed to be a certain sign that the devil had fought for her soul and had conquered. It could not be that she should be so terribly wretched if she were not also very wicked. She would tremble now at every sound; and though she still curled her lips, and poured scorn upon Peter from her eyes, as she moved away at his approach, she was almost so far beaten as to be desirous to succumb. She must either succumb to her aunt and to him, or else she must fly. How was she to live without a word of sympathy from any human being?

She had been careful to say little or nothing to Tetchen, having some indistinct idea that Tetchen was a double traitor. That Tetchen had on one occasion been in league with Ludovic, she was sure; but she thought that since that the woman had been in league with Peter also. The league with Ludovic had been very wicked, but that might be forgiven. A league with Peter was a sin to be forgiven never; and therefore Linda had resolutely declined of late to hold any converse with Tetchen other than that which the affairs of the house demanded. When Tetchen, who in this matter was most unjustly treated, would make little attempts to regain the confidence of her young mistress, her efforts were met with a repellant silence. And thus there was no one in the house to whom Linda could speak. This at last became so dreadful to her, the desolation of her position was so complete, that she had learned to regret her sternness to Tetchen. As far as she could now see, there was no alliance between Tetchen and Peter; and it might be the case, she thought, that her suspicions had been unjust to the old woman.

One evening, about the beginning of November, when it had already become dark at that hour in which Peter would present himself in Madame Staubach's parlour, he had entered the room, as was usual with him; and, as usual, Linda had at once left it. Peter, as he passed her, had looked at her with more than his usual anger, with an aggravated bitterness of condemnation in his eyes. She had been weeping in silence before he had appeared, and she had no power left to throw back her scorn at him. Still weeping, she went up into her room, and throwing herself on her bed, began, in her misery, to cry aloud for mercy. Some end must be brought to this, or the burden on her shoulders would be heavier than she could bear. She had gone to the window for a moment as she entered the chamber, and had thrown one glance in despair over towards the Ruden Platz. But the night was dark, and full of rain, and had he been there she could not have seen him. There was no one to befriend her. Then she threw herself on the bed and wept aloud.

She was still lying there when there came a very low tap at the door. She started up and listened. She had heard no footfall on the stairs, and it was, she thought, impossible that any one should have come up without her hearing the steps. Peter Steinmarc creaked whenever he went along the passages, and neither did her aunt or Tetchen tread with feet as light as that. She sat up, and then the knock was repeated,—very low and very clear. She still paused a moment, resolving that nothing should frighten her,—nothing should startle her. No change that could come to her would, she thought, be a change for the worse. She hastened up from off the bed, and stood upon the floor. Then she gave the answer that is usual to such a summons. 'Come in,' she said. She spoke low, but with clear voice, so that her word might certainly be heard, but not be heard afar. She stood about ten feet from the door, and when she heard the lock turned, her heart was beating violently.

The lock was turned, and the door was ajar, but it was not opened. 'Linda,' said a soft voice—'Linda, will you speak to me?' Heavens and earth! It was Ludovic,—Ludovic in her aunt's house,—Ludovic at her chamber door,—Ludovic there, within the very penetralia of their abode, while her aunt and Peter Steinmarc were sitting in the chamber below! But she had resolved that in no event would she be startled. In making that resolve, had she not almost hoped that this would be the voice that should greet her?

She could not now again say, 'Come in,' and the man who had had the audacity to advance so far, was not bold enough to advance farther, though invited. She stepped quickly to the door, and, placing her hand upon the lock, knew not whether to close it against the intruder or to confront the man. 'There can be but a moment, Linda; will you not speak to me?' said her lover.

What could her aunt do to her?—what Peter Steinmarc?—what could the world do, worse than had been done already? They had told her that she was a castaway, and she had half believed it. In the moments of her deepest misery she had believed it. If that were so, how could she fall lower? Would it not be sweet to her to hear one word of kindness in her troubles, to catch one note that should not be laden with rebuke? She opened the door, and stood before him in the gloom of the passage.

'Linda,—dear, dearest Linda;'—and before she knew that he was so near her, he had caught her hand.

'Hush! they are below;—they will hear you.'

'No; I could be up among the rafters before any one could be on the first landing; and no one should hear a motion.' Linda, in her surprise, looked up through the darkness, as though she could see the passage of which he spoke in the narrowing stair amidst the roof. What a terrible man was this, who had come to her bedroom door, and could thus talk of escaping amidst the rafters!

'Why are you here?' she whispered.

'Because I love you better than the light of heaven. Because I would go through fire and water to be near you. Linda,—dearest Linda, is it not true that you are in sorrow?'

'Indeed yes,' she said, shaking her head, while she still left her hand in his.

'And shall I not find an escape for you?'

'No, no; that is impossible.'

'I will try at least,' said he.

'You can do nothing for me,—nothing.'

'You love me, Linda? Say that you love me.' She remained silent, but her hand was still within his grasp. She could not lie to him, and say that she loved him not. 'Linda, you are all the world to me. The sweetest music that I could hear would be one word to say that I am dear to you.' She said not a word, but he knew now that she loved him. He knew it well. It is the instinct of the lover to know that his mistress has given him her heart heartily, when she does not deny the gift with more than sternness,—with cold cruelty. Yes; he knew her secret now; and pulling her close to him by her hand, by her arm, he wound his own arm round her waist tightly, and pressed his face close to hers. 'Linda, Linda,—my own, my own!—O God! how happy I am!' She suffered it all, but spoke not a word. His hot kisses were rained upon her lips, but she gave him never a kiss in return. He pressed her with all the muscles of his body, and she simply bore the pressure, uncomplaining, uncomplying, hardly thinking, half conscious, almost swooning, hysterical, with blood rushing wildly to her heart, lost in an agony of mingled fear and love. 'Oh, Linda!—oh, my own one!' But the kisses were still raining on her lips, and cheek, and brow. Had she heard her aunt's footsteps on the stairs, had she heard the creaking shoes of Peter Steinmarc himself, she could hardly have moved to save herself from their wrath. The pressure of her lover's arms was very sweet to her, but still, through it all, there was a consciousness that, in her very knowledge of that sweetness, the devil was claiming his own. Now, in very truth, was she a castaway. 'My love, my life!' said Ludovic, 'there are but a few moments for us. What can I do to comfort you?' She was still in his arms, pressed closely to his bosom, not trusting at all to the support of her own legs. She made one little struggle to free herself, but it was in vain. She opened her lips to speak, but there came no sound from them. Then there came again upon her that storm of kisses, and she was bound round by his arm, as though she were never again to be loosened. The waters that fell upon her were sweeter than the rains of heaven; but she knew,—there was still enough of life in her to remember,—that they were foul with the sulphur and the brimstone of the pit of hell.

'Linda,' he said, 'I am leaving Nuremberg; will you go with me?' Go with him! whither was she to go? How was she to go? And this going that he spoke of? Was it not thus usually with castaways? If it were true that she was in very fact already a castaway, why should she not go with him? And yet she was half sure that any such going on her part was a thing quite out of the question. As an actor will say of himself when he declines some proffered character, she could not see herself in that part. Though she could tell herself that she was a castaway, a very child of the devil, because she could thus stand and listen to her lover at her chamber door, yet could she not think of the sin that would really make her so without an abhorrence which made that sin frightful to her. She was not allured, hardly tempted, by the young man's offer as he made it. And yet, what else was there for her to do? And if it were true that she was a castaway, why should she struggle to be better than others who were of the same colour with herself? 'Linda, say, will you be my wife?'

His wife! Oh, yes, she would be his wife,—if it were possible. Even now, in the moment of her agony, there came to her a vague idea that she might do him some service if she were his wife, because she had property of her own. She was ready to acknowledge to herself that her duty to him was stronger than her duty to that woman below who had been so cruel to her. She would be his wife, if it were possible, even though he should drag her through the mud of poverty and through the gutters of tribulation. Could she walk down to her aunt's presence this moment his real wife, she would do so, and bear all that could be said to her. Could this be so, that storm which had been bitter with brimstone from the lowest pit, would at once become sweet with the air of heaven. But how could this be? She knew that it could not be. Marriage was a thing difficult to be done, hedged in with all manner of impediments, hardly to be reached at all by such a one as her, unless it might be such a marriage as that proposed to her with Peter Steinmarc. For girls with sweet, loving parents, for the Fanny Heisses of the world, marriage might be made easy. It was all very well for Ludovic Valcarm to ask her to be his wife; but in asking he must have known that she could not if she would; and yet the sound of the word was sweet to her. If it might be so, even yet she would not be a castaway.

But she did not answer his question. Struggling hard to speak, she muttered some prayer to him that he would leave her. 'Say that you love me,' demanded Ludovic. The demand was only whispered, but the words came hot into her ears.

'I do love you,' she replied.

'Then you will go with me.'

'No, no! It is impossible.'

'They will make you take that man for your husband.'

'They shall never do that;—never,—never.' In making this assertion, Linda found strength to extricate herself from her lover's arms and to stand alone.

'And how shall I come to you again?' said Ludovic.

'You must not come again. You should not have come

now. I would not have been here had I thought it possible you would have come.'

'But, Linda——' and then he went on to show to her how very unsatisfactory a courtship theirs would be, if, now that they were together, nothing could be arranged as to their future meeting. It soon became clear to Linda that Ludovic knew everything that was going on in the house, and had learned it all from Tetchen. Tetchen at this moment was quite aware of his presence up-stairs, and was prepared to cough aloud, standing at the kitchen door, if any sign were made that either Steinmarc or Madame Staubach were about to leave the parlour. Though it had seemed to Linda that her lover had come to her through the darkness, aided by the powers thereof, the assistance which had really brought him there was simply that of the old cook down-stairs. It certainly was on the cards that Tetchen might help him again after the same fashion, but Ludovic felt that such help would be but of little avail unless Linda, now that she had acknowledged her love, would do something to help also. With Ludovic Valcarm it was quite a proper course of things that he should jump out of a boat, or disappear into the roof among the rafters, or escape across the tiles and down the spouts in the darkness, as preliminary steps in a love affair. But in this special love affair such movements could only be preliminary; and therefore, as he was now standing face to face with Linda, and as there certainly had been difficulties in achieving this position, he was anxious to make some positive use of it. And then, as he explained to Linda in very few words, he was about to leave Nuremberg, and go to Munich. She did not quite understand whether he was always to remain in Munich; nor did she think of inquiring how he was to earn his bread there. But it was his scheme, that she should go with him and that there they should be married. If she would meet him at the railway station in time for the early train, they certainly could reach Munich without impediment. Linda would find no difficulty in leaving the house. Tetchen would take care that even the door should be open for her.

Linda listened to it all, and by degrees the impossibility of her assenting to such iniquity became less palpable. And though the wickedness of the scheme was still manifest to her, though she felt that, were she to assent to it, she would, in doing so, give herself up finally, body and soul, to the Evil One, yet was she not angry with Ludovic for proposing it. Nay, loving him well enough before, she loved him the better as he pressed her to go with him. But she would not go. She had nothing to say but, No, no, no. It was impossible. She was conscious after a certain fashion that her legs would refuse to carry her to the railway station on such an errand, that her physical strength would have failed her, and that were she to make ever so binding a promise, when the morning came she would not be there. He had again taken her hand, and was using all his eloquence, still speaking in low whispers, when there was heard a cough,—not loud, but very distinct,—Tetchen's cough as she stood at the kitchen door. Ludovic Valcarm, though the necessity for movement was so close upon him, would not leave Linda's hand till he had again pressed a kiss upon her mouth. Now, at last, in this perilous moment, there was some slightest movement on Linda's lips, which he flattered himself he might take as a response. Then, in a moment, he was gone and her door was shut, and he was escaping, after his own fashion, into the darkness,—she knew not whither and she knew not how, except that there was a bitter flavour of brimstone about it all.

She seated herself at the foot of the bed lost in amazement. She must first think,—she was bound first to think, of his safety; and yet what in the way of punishment could they do to him comparable to the torments which they could inflict upon her? She listened, and she soon heard Peter Steinmarc creaking in the room below. Tetchen had coughed because Peter was as usual going to his room, but had Ludovic remained at her door no one would have been a bit the wiser. No doubt Ludovic, up among the rafters, was thinking the same thing; but there must be no renewal of their intercourse that night, and therefore Linda bolted her door. As she did so, she

swore to herself that she would not unbolt it again that
evening at Ludovic's request. No such encroaching
request was made to her. She sat for nearly an hour at
the foot of her bed, waiting, listening, fearing, thinking,
hoping,—hardly hoping, when another step was heard
on the stair and in the passage,—a step which she well
knew to be that of her aunt Charlotte. Then she arose,
and as her aunt drew near she pulled back the bolt and
opened the door. The little oil lamp which she held
threw a timid fitful light into the gloom, and Linda
looked up unconsciously into the darkness of the roof over
her head.

It had been her custom to return to her aunt's parlour
as soon as she heard Peter creaking in the room below,
and she had still meant to do so on this evening; but
hitherto she had been unable to move, or at any rate so to
compose herself as to have made it possible for her to go
into her aunt's presence. Had she not had the whole
world of her own love story to fill her mind and her
heart?

'Linda, I have been expecting you to come down to
me,' said her aunt, gravely.

'Yes, aunt Charlotte, and I was coming.'

'It is late now, Linda.'

'Then, if you please, I will go to bed,' said Linda, who
was by no means sorry to escape the necessity of returning to the parlour.

'I could not go to my rest,' said Madame Staubach,
'without doing my duty by seeing you and telling you
again, that it is very wicked of you to leave the room
whenever our friend enters it. Linda, do you ever think
of the punishment which pride will bring down upon
you?'

'It is not pride.'

'Yes, Linda. It is the worst pride in the world.'

'I will sit with him all the evening if he will promise me
never again to ask me to be his wife.'

'The time will perhaps come, Linda, when you will be
only too glad to take him, and he will tell you that you
are not fit to be the wife of an honest man.' Then, having

uttered this bitter curse,—for such it was,—Madame
Staubach went across to her own room.

Linda, as she knelt at her bedside, tried to pray that
she might be delivered from temptation, but she felt that
her prayers were not prayers indeed. Even when she was
on her knees, with her hands clasped together as though
towards her God, her very soul was full of the presence
of that arm which had been so fast wound round her
waist. And when she was in bed she gave herself up to
the sweetness of her love. With what delicious violence
had that storm of kisses fallen on her! Then she prayed
for him, and strove very hard that her prayer might be
sincere.

CHAPTER VII

ANOTHER month had passed by, and it was now nearly
mid-winter. Another month had passed by, and
neither had Madame Staubach nor Peter Steinmarc
heard ought of Ludovic's presence among the rafters;
but things were much altered in the red house, and
Linda's life was hot, fevered, suspicious, and full of a
dangerous excitement. Twice again she had seen Ludovic, once meeting him in the kitchen, and once she had
met him at a certain dark gate in the Nonnen Garten, to
which she had contrived to make her escape for half an
hour on a false plea. Things were much changed with
Linda Tressel when she could condescend to do this. And
she had received from her lover a dozen notes, always
by the hand of Tetchen, and had written to him more
than once a few short, incoherent, startling words, in which
she would protest that she loved him, and protest also at
the same time that her love must be all in vain. 'It is of
no use. Do not write, and pray do not come. If this goes
on it will kill me. You know that I shall never give
myself to anybody else.' This was in answer to a proposition made through Tetchen that he should come again
to her,—should come, and take her away with him. He
had come, and there had been that interview in the
kitchen, but he had not succeeded in inducing her to
leave her home.

There had been many projects discussed between them, as to which Tetchen had given much advice. It was Tetchen's opinion, that if Linda would declare to her aunt that she meant at once to marry Ludovic Valcarm, and make him master of the house in which they lived, Madame Staubach would have no alternative but to submit quietly; that she would herself go forth and instruct the clergyman to publish the banns, and that Linda might thus become Valcarm's acknowledged wife before the snow was off the ground. Ludovic seemed to have his doubts about this, still signifying his preference for a marriage at Munich. When Tetchen explained to him that Linda would lose her character by travelling with him to Munich before she was his wife, he merely laughed at such an old wife's tale. Had not he himself seen Fanny Heisse and Max Bogen in the train together between Augsburg and Nuremberg long before they were married, and who had thought of saying a word against Fanny's character? 'But everybody knew about that,' said Linda. 'Let everybody know about this,' said Ludovic.

But Linda would not go. She would not go, even though Ludovic told her that it was imperative that he himself should quit Nuremberg. Such matters were in training,—he did not tell her what matters,—as would make his going quite imperative. Still she would take no step towards going with him. That advice of Tetchen's was much more in accordance with her desires. If she could act upon that, then she might have some happiness before her. She thought that she could make up her mind, and bring herself to declare her purpose to her aunt, if Ludovic would allow her to do so. But Ludovic declared that this could not be done, as preparatory to their being married at Nuremberg; and at last he was almost angry with her. Did she not trust him? Oh, yes, she would trust him with everything; with her happiness, her heart, her house,—with all that the world had left for her. But there was still that feeling left within her bosom, that if she did this thing which he proposed, she would be trusting him with her very soul.

Ludovic said a word to her about the house, and
Tetchen said many words. When Linda expressed an
opinion, that though the house might not belong to her
aunt legally, it was or ought to be her aunt's property in
point of honour, Tetchen only laughed at her. 'Don't let
her bother you about Peter then, if she chooses to live
here on favour,' said Tetchen. As Linda came to think
of it, it did appear hard to her that she should be tormented about Peter Steinmarc in her own house. She was not
Madame Staubach's child, nor her slave; nor, indeed,
was she of childish age. Gradually the idea grew upon
her that she might assert her right to free herself from the
tyranny to which she was made subject. But there was
always joined to this a consciousness, that though, according to the laws of the world, she might assert her right,
and claim her property, and acknowledge to everybody
her love to Ludovic Valcarm, she could do none of these
things in accordance with the laws of God. She had
become subject to her aunt by the circumstances of her
life, as though her aunt were in fact her parent, and the
fifth commandment was as binding on her as though she
were in truth the daughter of the guardian who had had
her in charge since her infancy. Once she said a word to
her aunt about the house, and was struck with horror by
the manner in which Madame Staubach had answered
her. She had simply said that, as the house was partly
hers, she had thought that she might suggest the expedi-
ency of getting another lodger in place of Peter Steinmarc.
But Madame Staubach had arisen from her chair and
had threatened to go at once out into the street,—'bare,
naked, and destitute,' as she expressed herself. 'If you
ever tell me again,' said Madame Staubach, 'that the
house is yours, I will never eat another meal beneath
your father's roof.' Linda, shocked at her own wickedness, had fallen at her aunt's knees, and promised that
she would never again be guilty of such wickedness. And
as she reflected on what she had done, she did believe
herself to have been very mean and very wicked. She
had known all her life that, though the house was hers
to live in, it was subject to the guidance of her aunt; and

so had she been subject till she had grown to be a woman. She could not quite understand that such subjection for the whole term of her life need be a duty to her; but when was the term of duty to be completed?

Between her own feelings on one side, and Tetchen's continued instigation on the other, she became aware that that which she truly needed was advice. These secret interviews and this clandestine correspondence were terrible to her very soul. She would not even yet be a castaway if it might be possible to save herself! There were two things fixed for her,—fixed, even though by their certainty she must become a castaway. She would never marry Peter Steinmarc, and she would never cease to love Ludovic Valcarm. But might it be possible that these assured facts should be reconciled to duty? If only there were somebody whom she might trust to tell her that!

Linda's father had had many friends in Nuremberg, and she could still remember those whom, as a child, she had seen from time to time in her father's house. The names of some were still familiar to her, and the memories of the faces even of one or two who had suffered her to play at their knees when she was little more than a baby, were present to her. Manners had so changed at the red house since those days, that few, if any, of these alliances had been preserved. The peculiar creed of Madame Staubach was not popular with the burghers of Nuremberg, and we all know how family friendships will die out when they are not kept alive by the warmth of familiar intercourse. There were still a few, and they among those most respected in the city, who would bow to Madame Staubach when they met her in the streets, and would smile and nod at Linda as they remembered the old days when they would be merry with a decorous mirth in the presence of her father. But there were none in the town,—no, not one,—who could interfere as a friend in the affairs of the widow Staubach's household, or who ever thought of asking Linda to sit at a friendly hearth. Close neighbourhood and school acquaintance had made Fanny Heisse her friend, but it was very rarely indeed that she had set her foot over the threshold of Jacob's door. Peter Steinmarc was their only friend, and his friendship had arisen from the mere fact of his residence beneath the same roof. It was necessary that their house should be divided with another, and in this way Peter had become their lodger. Linda certainly could not go to Peter for advice. She would have gone to Jacob Heisse, but that Jacob was a man slow of speech, somewhat timid in all matters beyond the making of furniture, and but little inclined to meddle with things out of his own reach. She fancied that the counsel which she required should be sought for from some one wiser and more learned than Jacob Heisse.

Among the names of those who had loved her father, which still rested in her memory, was that of Herr Molk, a man much spoken of in Nuremberg, one rich and of great repute, who was or had been burgomaster, and who occupied a house on the Egidien Platz, known to Linda well, because of its picturesque beauty. Even Peter Steinmarc, who would often speak of the town magistrates as though they were greatly inferior to himself in municipal lore and general wisdom, would mention the name of Herr Molk with almost involuntary respect. Linda had seen him from time to time either in the Platz or on the market-place, and her father's old friend had always smiled on her and expressed some hope that she was well and happy. Ah, how vain had been that hope! What if she should now go to Herr Molk and ask him for advice? She would not speak to Tetchen, because Tetchen would at once tell it all to Ludovic; and in this matter, as Linda felt, she must not act as Ludovic would bid her. Yes; she would go to this noted pundit of the city, and, if he would allow her so to do, would tell to him all her story.

And then she made another resolve. She would not do this without informing her aunt that it was about to be done. On this occasion, even though her aunt should tell her to remain in the house, she would go forth. But her aunt should not throw it in her teeth that she had acted on the sly. One day, one cold November morning, when the hour of their early dinner was approaching, she went up-stairs from the kitchen for her hat and cloak, and then, equipped for her walk, presented herself before her aunt.

'Linda, where are you going?' demanded Madame Staubach.

'I am going, aunt Charlotte, to Herr Molk, in the Egidien Platz.'

'To Herr Molk? And why? Has he bidden you come to him?' Then Linda told her story, with much difficulty. She was unhappy, she said, and wanted advice. She remembered this man,—that he was the friend of her father. 'I am sorry, Linda, that you should want other advice than that which I can give you.'

'Dear aunt, it is just that. You want me to marry this man here, and I cannot do it. This has made you miserable, and me miserable. Is it not true that we are not happy as we used to be?'

'I certainly am not happy. How can I be happy when I see you wandering astray? How can I be happy when you tell me that you love the man in Nuremberg whom I believe of all to be most wicked and ungodly? How can I be happy when you threaten to expel from the house, because it is your own, the only man whom I love, honour, and respect?'

'I never said so, aunt Charlotte;—I never thought of saying such a thing.'

'And what will you ask of this stranger should you find yourself in his presence?'

'I will tell him everything, and ask him what I should do.'

'And will you tell him truly?'

'Certainly, aunt Charlotte; I will tell him the truth in everything.'

'And if he bids you marry the man whom I have chosen as your husband?' Linda, when this suggestion was made to her, became silent. Truly it was impossible that any wise man in Nuremberg could tell her that such a sacrifice as that was necessary! Then Madame Staubach repeated the question. 'If he bids you marry Peter Steinmarc, will you do as he bids you?'

Surely she would not be so bidden by her father's friend! 'I will endeavour to do as he bids me,' said Linda.

'Then go to him, my child, and may God so give him grace that he may soften the hardness of your heart, and prevail with you to put down beneath your feet the temptations of Satan; and that he may quell the spirit of evil within you. God forbid that I should think that there is no wisdom in Nuremberg fitter than mine to guide you. If the man be a man of God, he will give you good counsel.'

Then Linda, wondering much at her aunt's ready acquiescence, went forth, and walked straightway to the house of Herr Molk in the Egidien Platz.

CHAPTER VIII

A WALK of ten minutes took Linda from the Schutt island to the Egidien Platz, and placed her before the door of Herr Molk's house. The Egidien Platz is, perhaps, the most fashionable quarter of Nuremberg, if Nuremberg may be said to have a fashion in such matters. It is near to the Rathhaus, and to St. Sebald's Church, and is not far distant from the old Burg or Castle in which the Emperors used to dwell when they visited the imperial city of Nuremberg. This large open Place has a church in its centre, and around it are houses almost all large, built with gables turned towards the street, quaint, picturesque, and eloquent of much burghers' wealth. There could be no such square in a city which was not or had not been very rich. And among all the houses in the Egidien Platz, there was no house to exceed in beauty of ornament, in quaintness of architecture, or in general wealth and comfort, that which was inhabited by Herr Molk.

Linda stood for a moment at the door, and then putting up her hand, pulled down the heavy iron bell-handle, which itself was a gem of art, representing some ancient and discreet burgher of the town, wrapped in his cloak, and almost hidden by his broad-brimmed hat. She heard the bell clank close inside the door, and then the portal was open, as though the very pulling of the bell had opened it. The lock at least was open, so that Linda could push the door with her hand and enter over the threshold. This she did, and she found herself within a long narrow court or yard, round which, one above another, there ran galleries, open to the court, and guarded with heavy balustrades of carved wood. From the narrowness of the enclosure, the house on each side seemed to be very high, and Linda, looking round with astonished eyes, could see that at every point the wood was carved. And the waterspouts were ornamented with grotesque figures, and the huge broad stairs which led to the open galleries on the left hand were of polished oak, made so slippery with the polishers' daily care that it was difficult to tread upon them without falling. All around the bottom of the court there were open granaries or warehouses; for there seemed to be nothing that could be called a room on the ground floor, beyond the porter's lodge; and these open warehouses seemed to be filled full with masses of stacked firewood. Linda knew well the value of such stores in Nuremberg, and lost none of her veneration for Herr Molk because of such nature were the signs of his domestic wealth.

As she timidly looked around her she saw an old woman within the gate of the porter's lodge, and inquired whether Herr Molk was at home and disengaged. The woman simply motioned her to the wicket gate by which the broad polished stairs were guarded. Linda, hesitating to advance into so grand a mansion alone, and yet knowing that she should do as she was bidden, entered the wicket and ascended carefully to the first gallery. Here was another bell ready to her hand, the handle of which consisted of a little child in iron-work. This also she pulled, and waited till some one should come. Presently there was a scuffling heard of quick feet in the gallery, and three children ran up to her. In the middle was the elder, a girl dressed in dark silk, and at her sides

were two boys habited in black velvet. They all had long
fair hair, and large blue eyes, and soft peach-like cheeks,
—such as those who love children always long to kiss.
Linda thought that she had never seen children so
gracious and so fair. She asked again whether Herr Molk
was at home, and at liberty to see a stranger. 'Quite a
stranger,' said poor Linda, with what emphasis she could
put upon her words. The little girl said that her grand-
father was at home, and would see any visitor,—as a
matter of course. Would Linda follow her? Then the
child, still leading her little brothers, tripped up the
stairs to the second gallery, and opening a door which led
into one of the large front rooms, communicated to an
old gentleman who seemed to be taking exercise in the
apartment with his hands behind his back, that he was
wanted by a lady.

'Wanted, am I, my pretty one? Well, and here I am.'
Then the little girl, giving a long look up into Linda's
face, retreated, taking her brothers with her, and closing
the door. Thus Linda found herself in the room along
with the old gentleman, who still kept his hands behind
his back. It was a singular apartment, nearly square, but
very large, panelled with carved wood, not only throughout the walls, but up to the ceiling also. And the floor
was polished even brighter than were the stairs. Herr
Molk must have been well accustomed to take his exercise there, or he would surely have slipped and fallen in
his course. There was but one small table in the room,
which stood unused near a wall, and there were perhaps
not more than half-a-dozen chairs,—all high-backed,
covered with old tapestry, and looking as though they
could hardly have been placed there for ordinary use.
On one of these, Linda sat at the old man's bidding; and
he placed himself on another, with his hands still behind
him, just seating himself on the edge of the chair.

'I am Linda Tressel,' said poor Linda. She saw at a
glance that she herself would not have known Herr Molk,
whom she had never before met without his hat, and she
perceived also that he had not recognised her.

'Linda Tressel! So you are. Dear, dear! I knew your

father well,—very well. But, lord, how long that is ago!
He is dead ever so many years; how many years?'

'Sixteen years,' said Linda.

'Sixteen years dead! And he was a younger man than
I,—much younger. Let me see,—not so much younger,
but younger. Linda Tressel, your father's daughter is
welcome to my house. A glass of wine will not hurt you
this cold weather.' She declined the wine, but the old
man would have his way. He went out, and was absent
perhaps five minutes. Then he returned bearing a small
tray in his own hands, with a long-necked bottle and
glasses curiously engraved, and he insisted that Linda
should clink her glass with his. 'And now, my dear,
what is it that I can do for you?'

So far Linda's mission had prospered well; but now
that the story was to be told, she found very much difficulty in telling it. She had to begin with the whole
history of the red house, and of the terms upon which her
aunt had come to reside in it. She had one point at least
in her favour. Herr Molk was an excellent listener. He
would nod his head, and pat one hand upon the other,
and say, 'Yes, yes,' without the slightest sign of im-
patience. It seemed as though he had no other care
before him than that of listening to Linda's story. When
she experienced the encouragement which came from the
nodding of his head and the patting of his hand, she went
on boldly. She told how Peter Steinmarc had come to the
house, and how her aunt was a woman peculiar from
the strength of her religious convictions. 'Yes, my dear,
yes; we know that,—we know that,' said Herr Molk.
Linda did her best to say nothing evil of her aunt. Then
she came to the story of Peter's courtship. 'He is quite
an old man, you know,' said poor Linda, thoughtfully.
Then she was interrupted by Herr Molk. 'A worthy
man; I know him well,—well,—well. Peter Steinmarc
is our clerk at the Rathhaus. A very worthy man is Peter
Steinmarc. Your father, my dear, was clerk at the
Rathhaus, and Peter followed him. He is not young,—
not just young; but a very worthy man. Go on, my dear.'
Linda had resolved to tell it all, and she did tell it all.

It was difficult to tell, but it all came out. Perhaps there could be no listener more encouraging to such a girl as Linda than the patient, gentle-mannered old man with whom she was closeted. 'She had a lover whom she loved dearly,' she said,—'a young man.'

'Oh, a lover,' said Herr Molk. But there seemed to be no anger in his voice. He received the information as though it were important, but not astonishing. Then Linda even told him how the lover had come across the river on the Sunday morning, and how it had happened that she had not told her aunt, and how angry her aunt had been. 'Yes, yes,' said Herr Molk; 'it is better that your elders should know such things,—always better. But go on, my dear.' Then she told also how the lover had come down, or had gone up, through the rafters, and the old man smiled. Perhaps he had hidden himself among rafters fifty years ago, and had some sweet remembrance of the feat. And now Linda wanted to know what was she to do, and how she ought to act. The house was her own, but she would not for worlds drive her aunt out of it. She loved her lover very dearly, and she could not love Peter Steinmarc at all,—not in that way.

'Has the young man means to support a wife?' asked Herr Molk. Linda hesitated, knowing that there was still a thing to be told, which she had not as yet dared to mention. She knew too that it must be told. Herr Molk, as she hesitated, asked a second question on this very point. 'And what is the young man's name, my dear? It all depends on his name and character, and whether he has means to support a wife.'

'His name——is——Ludovic Valcarm,' said Linda, whispering the words very low.

The old man jumped from his seat with an alacrity that Linda had certainly not expected. 'Ludovic—Valcarm!' he said; 'why, my dear, the man is in prison this moment. I signed the committal yesterday myself.'

'In prison!' said Linda, rising also from her chair.

'He is a terrible young man,' said Herr Molk—'a very terrible young man. He does all manner of things;—I can't explain what. My dear young woman, you must not think of taking Ludovic Valcarm for your husband; you must not, indeed. You had better make up your mind to take Peter Steinmarc. Peter Steinmarc can support a wife, and is very respectable. I have known Peter all my life. Ludovic Valcarm! Oh dear! That would be very bad,—very bad indeed!'

Linda's distress was excessive. It was not only that the tidings which she heard of Ludovic were hard to bear, but it seemed that Herr Molk was intent on ranging himself altogether with her enemies respecting Peter Steinmarc. In fact, the old man's advice to her respecting Peter was more important in her mind that his denunciation of Ludovic. She did not quite credit what he said of Ludovic. It was doubtless true that Ludovic was in prison; probably for some political offence. But such men, she thought, were not kept in prison long. It was bad, this fact of her lover's imprisonment; but not so bad as the advice which her counsellor gave her, and which she knew she would be bound to repeat to her aunt.

'But, Herr Molk, sir, if I do not love Peter Steinmarc —if I hate him——?'

'Oh, my dear, my dear! This is a terrible thing. There is not such another ne'er-do-well in all Nuremberg as Ludovic Valcarm. Support a wife! He cannot support himself. And it will be well if he does not die in a jail. Oh dear! oh dear! For your father's sake, fraulein—for your father's sake, I would go any distance to save you from this. Your father was a good man, and a credit to the city. And Peter Steinmarc is a good man.'

'But I need not marry Peter Steinmarc, Herr Molk.'

'You cannot do better, my dear,—indeed you cannot. See what your aunt says. And remember, my dear, that you should submit yourself to your elders and your betters. Peter is not so old. He is not old at all. I was one of the city magistrates when Peter was a little boy. I remember him well. And he began life in your father's office. Nothing can be more respectable than he has been. And then Ludovic Valcarm! oh dear! If you ask my advice, I should counsel you to accept Peter Steinmarc.'

There was nothing more to be got from Herr Molk.

And with this terrible recommendation still sounding in her ears, Linda sadly made her way back from the Egidien Platz to the Schütt island.

CHAPTER IX

LINDA TRESSEL, as she returned home to the house in the Schütt island, became aware that it was necessary for her to tell to her aunt all that had passed between herself and Herr Molk. She had been half stunned with grief as she left the magistrate's house, and for a while had tried to think that she could keep back from Madame Staubach at any rate the purport of the advice that had been given to her. And as she came to the conclusion that this would be impossible to her,—that it must all come out, —various wild plans flitted across her brain. Could she not run away without returning to the red house at all? But whither was she to run, and with whom? The only one who would have helped her in this wild enterprise had been sent to prison by that ill-conditioned old man who had made her so miserable! At this moment, there was no longer any hope in her bosom that she should save herself from being a castaway; nay, there was hardly a wish. There was no disreputable life so terrible to her thoughts, no infamy so infamous in idea to her, as would be respectability in the form of matrimony with Peter Steinmarc. And now, as she walked along painfully, going far out of her way that she might have some little time for reflection, turning all this in her mind, she began almost to fear that if she went back to her aunt, her aunt would prevail, and that in very truth Peter Steinmarc would become her lord and master. Then there was another plan, as impracticable as that scheme of running away. What if she were to become sullen, and decline to speak at all? She was well aware that in such a contest her aunt's tongue would be very terrible to her; and as the idea crossed her mind, she told herself that were she so to act people would treat her as a mad woman. But even that, she thought, would be better than being forced to marry Peter Steinmarc. Before she had reached the island, she knew that the one scheme was as impossible as the other. She entered the house very quietly, and turning to the left went at once into the kitchen.

'Linda, your aunt is waiting dinner for you this hour,' said Tetchen.

'Why did you not take it to her by herself?' said Linda, crossly.

'How could I do that, when she would not have it? You had better go in now at once. But, Linda, does anything ail you?'

'Very much ails me,' said Linda.

Then Tetchen came close to her, and whispered, 'Have you heard anything about him?'

'What have you heard, Tetchen? Tell me at once.'

'He is in trouble.'

'He is in prison!' Linda said this with a little hysteric scream. Then she began to sob and cry, and turned her back to Tetchen and hid her face in her hands.

'I have heard that too,' said Tetchen. 'They say the burgomasters have caught him with letters on him from some terrible rebels up in Prussia, and that he has been plotting to have the city burned down. But I don't believe all that, fraulein.'

'He is in prison. I know he is in prison,' said Linda. 'I wish I were there too;—so I do, or dead. I'd rather be dead.' Then Madame Staubach, having perhaps heard the lock of the front door when it was closed, came into the kitchen. 'Linda,' she said, 'I am waiting for you.

'I do not want any dinner,' said Linda, still standing with her face turned to the wall. Then Madame Staubach took hold of her arm, and led her across the passage into the parlour. Linda said not a word as she was being thus conducted, but was thinking whether it might not even yet serve her purpose to be silent and sullen. She was still sobbing, and striving to repress her sobs; but she allowed herself to be led without resistance, and in an instant the door was closed, and she was seated on the old sofa with her aunt beside her.

'Have you seen Herr Molk?' demanded Madame Staubach.

'Yes; I have seen him.'

'And what has he said to you?' Then Linda was silent. 'You told me that you would seek his counsel; and that you would act as he might advise you.'

'No; I did not say that.'

'Linda!'

'I did not promise. I made no promise.'

'Linda, surely you did promise. When I asked you whether you would do as he might bid you, you said that you would be ruled by him. Then, knowing that he is wise, and of repute in the city, I let you go. Linda, was it not so?' Linda could not remember what words had in truth been spoken between them. She did remember that in her anxiety to go forth, thinking it to be impossible that the burgomaster should ask her to marry a man old enough to be her father, she had in some way assented to her aunt's proposition. But yet she thought that she had made no definite promise that she would marry the man she hated. She did not believe that she would absolutely have promised that under any possible circumstances she would do so. She could not, however, answer her aunt's question; so she continued to sob, and endeavoured again to hide her face. 'Did you tell the man everything, my child?' demanded Madame Staubach.

'Yes, I did.'

'And what has he said to you?'

'I don't know.'

'You don't know! Linda, that cannot be true. It is not yet half an hour since, and you do not know what Herr Molk said to you? Did you tell him of my wish about our friend Peter?'

'Yes, I did.'

'And did you tell him of your foolish fancy for that wicked young man?'

'Yes, I did.'

'And what did he say?'

Linda was still silent. It was almost impossible for her to tell her aunt what the man had said to her. She could not bring herself to tell the story of what had passed in the panelled room. Had Madame Staubach been in any

way different from what she was,—had she been at all
less stubborn, less hard, less reliant on the efficacy of her
religious convictions to carry her over all obstacles,—she
would have understood something of the sufferings of the
poor girl with whom she was dealing. But with her the
only idea present to her mind was the absolute necessity
of saving Linda from the wrath to come by breaking her
spirit in regard to things of this world, and crushing her
into atoms here, that those atoms might be remoulded in
a form that would be capable of a future and a better
life. Instead therefore of shrinking from cruelty, Madame
Staubach was continually instigating herself to be cruel.
She knew that the image of the town-clerk was one
simply disgusting to Linda, and therefore she was determined to force that image upon her. She knew that the
girl's heart was set upon Ludovic Valcarm with all the
warmth of its young love, and therefore she conceived it
to be her duty to prove to the girl that Ludovic Valcarm
was one already given up to Satan and Satanic agencies.
Linda must be taught not only to acknowledge, but in
very fact to understand and perceive, that this world is a
vale of tears, that its paths are sharp to the feet, and that
they who walk through it should walk in mourning and
tribulation. What though her young heart should be
broken by the lesson,—be broken after the fashion in
which human hearts are made to suffer? To Madame
Staubach's mind a broken heart and a contrite spirit
were pretty much the same thing. It was good that
hearts should be broken, that all the inner humanities
of the living being should be, as it were, crushed on a
wheel and ground into fragments, so that nothing should
be left capable of receiving pleasure from the delights of
this world. Such, according to her theory of life, was the
treatment to which young women should be subjected.
The system needed for men might probably be different.
It was necessary that they should go forth and work; and
Madame Staubach conceived it to be possible that the
work of the world could not be adequately done by men
who had been subjected to the crushing process which
was requisite for women. Therefore it was that she

admitted Peter Steinmarc to her confidence as a worthy
friend, though Peter was by no means a man enfranchised from the thralls of the earth. Of young women
there was but one with whom she could herself deal; but
in regard to that one Madame Staubach was resolved
that no softness of heart should deter her from her duty.
'Linda,' she said, after pausing for a while, 'I desire to
know from you what Herr Molk has said to you!' Then
there was a short period of silence. 'Linda, did he sanction your love for Ludovic Valcarm?'

'No,' said Linda, sullenly.

'I should think not, indeed! And, Linda, did he bid
you be rebellious in that other matter?'

Linda paused again before she answered; but it was
but for a moment, and then she replied, in the same
voice, 'No.'

'Did he tell you that you had better take Peter Steinmarc for your husband?' Linda could not bring herself
to answer this, but sat beating the floor with her foot,
and with her face turned away and her eyes fixed upon
the wall. She was no longer sobbing now, but was
hardening herself against her aunt. She was resolving
that she would be a castaway,—that she would have
nothing more to do with godliness, or even with decency.
She had found godliness and decency too heavy to be
borne. In all her life, had not that moment in which
Ludovic had held her tight bound by his arm round her
waist been the happiest? Had it not been to her, her one
single morsel of real bliss? She was thinking now whether
she would fly round upon her aunt and astonish her
tyrant by a declaration of principles that should be
altogether new. Then came the question again in the
same hard voice, 'Did he not tell you that you had better
take Peter Steinmarc for your husband?'

'I won't take Peter Steinmarc for my husband,' said
Linda; and she did in part effect that flying round of
which she had been thinking. 'I won't take Peter Steinmarc for my husband, let the man say what he may.
How can I marry him if I hate him? He is a—beast.'

Then Madame Staubach groaned. Linda had often

heard her groan, but had never known her to groan as
she groaned now. It was very deep and very low, and
prolonged with a cadence that caused Linda to tremble
in every limb. And Linda understood it thoroughly. It
was as though her aunt had been told by an angel that
Satan was coming to her house in person that day. And
Linda did that which the reader also should do. She gave
to her aunt full credit for pure sincerity in her feelings.
Madame Staubach did believe that Satan was coming
for her niece, if not actually come; he was close at hand,
if not arrived. The crushing, if done at all, must be done
instantly, so that Satan should find the spirit so broken
and torn to paltry fragments as not to be worth his
acceptance. She stretched forth her hand and took hold
of her niece. 'Linda,' she said, 'do you ever think of the
bourne to which the wicked ones go;—they who are
wicked as you now are wicked?'

'I cannot help it,' said Linda.

'And did he not bid you take this man for your husband?'

'I will not do his bidding, then! It would kill me. Do
you not know that I love Ludovic better than all the
world? He is in prison, but shall I cease to love him for
that reason? He came to me once up-stairs at night when
you were sitting here with that—beast, and I swore to
him then that I would never love another man,—that I
should never marry anybody else!'

'Came to you once up-stairs at night! To your own
chamber?'

'Yes, he did. You may know all about it, if you please.
You may know everything. I don't want anything to be
secret. He came to me, and when he had his arms round
me I told him that I was his own,—his own,—his own.
How can I be the wife of another man after that?'

Madame Staubach was so truly horrified by what she
had first heard, was so astonished, that she omitted even
to groan. Valcarm had been with this wretched girl up
in her own chamber! She hardly even now believed that
which it seemed to her that she was called upon to believe,
having never as yet for a moment doubted the real purity

of her niece even when she was most vehemently denouncing her as a reprobate, a castaway, and a child of Satan. The reader will know to what extent Linda had been imprudent, to what extent she had sinned. But Madame Staubach did not know. She had nothing to guide her but the words of this poor girl who had been so driven to desperation by the misery which enveloped her, that she almost wished to be taken for worse than she was in order that she might escape the terrible doom from which she saw no other means of escape. Nobody, it is true, could have forced her to marry Peter Steinmarc. There was no law, no custom in Nuremberg, which would have assisted her aunt, or Peter, or even the much-esteemed and venerable Herr Molk himself, in compelling her to submit to such nuptials. She was free to exercise her own choice, if only she had had strength to assert her freedom. But youth, which rebels so often against the authority and wisdom of age, is also subject to much tyranny from age. Linda did not know the strength of her own position, had not learned to recognise the fact of her own individuality. She feared the power of her aunt over her, and through her aunt the power of the man whom she hated; and she feared the now provoked authority of Herr Molk, who had been with her weak as a child is weak, counselling her to submit herself to a suitor unfitted for her, because another man who loved her was also unfit. And, moreover, Linda, though she was now willing in her desperation to cast aside all religious scruples of her own, still feared those with which her aunt was armed. Unless she did something, or at least said something, to separate herself entirely from her aunt, this terrible domestic tyrant would overcome her by the fear of denunciation, which would terrify her soul even though she had dared to declare to herself that in her stress of misery she would throw overboard all consideration of her soul's welfare. Though she intended no longer to live in accordance with her religious belief, she feared what religion could say to her,—dreaded to the very marrow of her bones the threats of God's anger and of Satan's power with which her aunt would harass her. If only she could rid herself of it all!

Therefore, though she perceived that the story which she had told of herself had filled her aunt's mind with a horrible and a false suspicion, she said nothing to correct the error. Therefore she said nothing further, though her aunt sat looking at her with open mouth, and eyes full of terror, and hands clasped, and pale cheeks.

'In this house,—in this very house!' said Madame Staubach, not knowing what it might best become her to say in such a strait as this.

'The house is as much mine as yours,' said Linda, sullenly. And she too, in saying this, had not known what she meant to say, or what she ought to have said. Her aunt had alluded to the house, and there seemed to her, in her distress, to be something in that on which she could hang a word.

For a while her aunt sat in silence looking at Linda, and then she fell upon her knees, with her hands clasped to heaven. What was the matter of her prayers we may not here venture to surmise; but, such as they were, they were sincere. Then she arose and went slowly as far as the door, but she returned before she had reached the threshold. 'Wretched child!' she said.

'Yes, you have made me wretched,' said Linda.

'Listen to me, Linda, if so much grace is left to you. After what you have told me, I cannot but suppose that all hope of happiness or comfort in this world is over both for you and me.'

'For myself, I wish I were dead,' said Linda.

'Have you no thought of what will come after death? Oh, my child, repentance is still possible to you, and with repentance there will come at length grace and salvation. Mary Magdalene was blessed,—was specially blessed among women.'

'Pshaw!' said Linda, indignantly. What had she to do with Mary Magdalene? The reality of her position then came upon her, and not the facts of that position which she had for a moment almost endeavoured to simulate.

'Do you not hate yourself for what you have done?'

'No, no, no. But I hate Peter Steinmarc, and I hate Herr Molk, and if you are so cruel to me I shall hate you.

I have done nothing wrong. I could not help it if he came up-stairs. He came because he loved me, and because you would not let him come in a proper way. Nobody else loves me, but he would do anything for me. And now they have thrown him into prison!'

The case was so singular in all its bearings, that Madame Staubach could make nothing of it. Linda seemed to have confessed her iniquity, and yet, after her confession, spoke of herself as though she were the injured person,—of herself and her lover as though they were both ill used. According to Madame Staubach's own ideas, Linda ought now to have been in the dust, dissolved in tears, wiping the floor with her hair, utterly subdued in spirit, hating herself as the vilest of God's creatures. But there was not even an outward sign of contrition. And then, in the midst of all this real tragedy, Tetchen brought in the dinner. The two women sat down together, but neither of them spoke a word. Linda did eat something,—a morsel or two; but Madame Staubach would not touch the food on the table. Then Tetchen was summoned to take away the all but unused plates. Tetchen, when she saw how it had been, said nothing, but looked from the face of one to the face of the other. 'She has heard all about that scamp Ludovic,' said Tetchen to herself, as she carried the dishes back into the kitchen.

It had been late when the dinner had been brought to them, and the dusk of the evening came upon them as soon as Tetchen's clatter with the crockery was done. Madame Staubach sat in her accustomed chair, with her eyes closed, and her hands clasped on her lap before her. A stranger might have thought that she was asleep, but Linda knew that her aunt was not sleeping. She also sat silent till she thought that the time was drawing near at which Steinmarc might probably enter the parlour. Then she arose to go, but could not leave her aunt without a word. 'Aunt Charlotte,' she said, 'I am ill,—very ill; my head is throbbing, and I will go to bed.' Madame Staubach merely shook her head, and shook her hands, and remained silent, with her eyes still closed. She had not even yet resolved upon the words with which it would be expedient that she should address her niece. Then Linda left the room, and went to her own apartment.

Madame Staubach, when she was alone, sobbed and cried, and knelt and prayed, and walked the length and breadth of the room in an agony of despair and doubt. She also was in want of a counsellor to whom she could go in her present misery. And there was no such counsellor. It seemed to her to be impossible that she should confide everything to Peter Steinmarc. And yet it was no more than honest that Peter should be told before he was allowed to continue his courtship. Even now, though she had seen Linda's misery, Madame Staubach thought that the marriage which she had been so anxious to arrange would be the safest way out of all their troubles,—if only Peter might be brought to consent to it after hearing all the truth. And she fancied that those traits in Peter's character, appearance, and demeanour which were so revolting to Linda would be additional means of bringing Linda back from the slough of despond,—if only such a marriage might still be possible. But the crushing must be more severe than had hitherto been intended, the weights imposed must be heavier, and the human atoms smaller and more like the dust.

While she was meditating on this there came the usual knock at the door, and Steinmarc entered the room. She greeted him, as was her wont, with but a word or two, and he sat down and lighted his pipe. An observant man might have known, even from the sound of her breathing, that something had stirred Madame Staubach more than usual. But Peter was not an observant man, and, having something on his own mind, paid but little attention to the widow. At last, having finished his first pipe and filled it again, he spoke. 'Madame Staubach,' he said, 'I have been thinking about Linda Tressel.'

'And so have I, Peter,' said Madame Staubach.

'Yes,—of course; that is natural. She is your niece, and you and she have interests in common.'

'What interests, Peter? Ah me! I wish we had.'

'Of course it is all right that you should, and I say nothing about that. But, Madame Staubach, I do not like to be made a fool of;—I particularly object to be made a fool of. If Linda is to become my wife, there is not any time to be lost.' Then Peter recommenced the smoking of his new-lighted pipe with great vigour.

Madame Staubach at this moment became a martyr to great scruples. Was it her duty, or was it not her duty, to tell Peter at this moment all that she had heard to-day? She rather thought that it was her duty to do so, and yet she was restrained by some feeling of feminine honour from disgracing her niece,—by some feeling of feminine honour for which she afterwards did penance with many inward flagellations of the spirit.

'You must not be too hard upon her, Peter,' said Madame Staubach with a trembling voice.

'It is all very well saying that, and I do not think that I am the man to be hard upon any one. But the fact is that this young woman has got a lover, which is a thing of which I do not approve. I do not approve of it at all, Madame Staubach. Some persons who stand very high indeed in the city,—indeed I may say that none in Nuremberg stand higher,—have asked me to-day whether I am engaged to marry Linda Tressel. What answer am I to make when I am so asked, Madame Staubach? One of our leading burgomasters was good enough to say that he hoped it was so for the young woman's sake.' Madame Staubach, little as she knew of the world of Nuremberg, was well aware who was the burgomaster. 'That is all very well, my friend; but if it be so that Linda will not renounce her lover,—who, by the by, is at this moment locked up in prison, so that he cannot do any harm just now,—why then, in that case, Madame Staubach, I must renounce her.' Having uttered these terrible words, Peter Steinmarc smoked away again with all his fury.

A fortnight ago, had Peter Steinmarc ventured to speak to her in this strain, Madame Staubach would have answered him with some feminine pride, and would have told him that her niece was not a suppliant for his hand.

This she did not dare to do now. She was all at fault as
to facts, and did not know what the personages of
Nuremberg might be saying in respect to Linda. Were
she to quarrel altogether with Steinmarc, she thought
that there would be left to her no means of bringing upon
Linda that salutary crushing which alone might be
efficacious for her salvation. She was therefore compelled
to temporise. Let Peter be silent for a week, and at the
end of that week let him speak again. If things could not
then be arranged to his satisfaction, Linda should be
regarded as altogether a castaway.

'Very well, Madame Staubach. Then I will ask her
for the last time this day week.' In coarsest sackcloth,
and with bitterest ashes, did Madame Staubach on that
night do spiritual penance for her own sins and for those
of Linda Tressel.

This week had nearly passed to the duration of which
Peter Steinmarc had assented, and at the end of which
it was to be settled whether Linda would renounce
Ludovic Valcarm, or Peter himself would renounce
Linda. With a manly propriety he omitted any spoken
allusion to the subject during those smoking visits which
he still paid on alternate days to the parlour of Madame
Staubach. But, though he said nothing, his looks and
features and the motions of his limbs were eloquent of
his importance and his dignity during this period of
waiting. He would salute Madame Staubach when he
entered the chamber with a majesty of demeanour which
he had not before affected, and would say a few words
on subjects of public interest—such as the weather, the
price of butter, and the adulteration of the city beer—in
false notes, in tones which did not belong to him, and
which in truth disgusted Madame Staubach, who was
sincere in all things. But Madame Staubach, though she
was disgusted, did not change her mind or abandon her
purpose. Linda was to be made to marry Peter Steinmarc,
not because he was a pleasant man, but because such a
discipline would be for the good of her soul. Madame
Staubach therefore listened, and said little or nothing;
and when Peter on a certain Thursday evening remarked

as he was leaving the parlour that the week would be over on the following morning, and that he would do himself the honour of asking for the fraulein's decision on his return from the town-hall at five P.M. on the morrow, apologising at the same time for the fact that he would then be driven to intrude on an irregular day, Madame Staubach merely answered by an assenting motion of her head, and by the utterance of her usual benison, 'God in His mercy be with you, Peter Steinmarc.' 'And with you too, Madame Staubach.' Then Peter marched forth with great dignity, holding his pipe as high as his shoulder.

Linda Tressel had kept her bed during nearly the whole week, and had in truth been very ill. Hitherto it had been her aunt's scheme of life to intermit in some slight degree the acerbity of her usual demeanour in periods of illness. At such times she would be very constant with the reading of good books by the bedside and with much ghostly advice to the sufferer, but she would not take it amiss if the patient succumbed to sleep while she was thus employed, believing sleep to be pardonable at such times of bodily weakness, and perhaps salutary; and she would be softer in her general manner, and would sometimes descend to the saying of tender little words, and would administer things agreeable to the palate which might at the same time be profitable to the health. So thus there had been moments in which Linda had felt that it would be comfortable to be always ill. But now, during the whole of this week, Madame Staubach had been very doubtful as to her conduct. At first it had seemed to her that all tenderness must be misplaced in circumstances so terrible, till there had been an actual resolution of repentance, till the spirit had been made to pass seven times through the fire, till the heart had lost all its human cords and fibres. But gradually, and that before the second day had elapsed, there came upon her a conviction that she had in some way mistaken the meaning of Linda's words, and that matters were not as she had supposed. She did not now in the least doubt Linda's truth. She was convinced that Linda had intentionally told no falsehood, and that she would tell none. But there were questions which she would not ask, which she could not ask at any rate except by slow degrees. Something, however, she learned from Tetchen, something from Linda herself, and thus there came upon her a conviction that there might be no frightful story to tell to Peter,—that in all probability there was no such story to be told. What she believed at this time was in fact about the truth.

But if it were as she believed, then was it the more incumbent on her to see that this marriage did not slip through her fingers. She became very busy, and in her eagerness she went to Herr Molk. Herr Molk had learned something further about Ludovic, and promised that he would himself come down and see 'the child.' He would see 'the child,' ill as she was, in bed, and perhaps say a word or two that might assist. Madame Staubach found that the burgomaster was quite prepared to advocate the Steinmarc marriage, being instigated thereto apparently by his civic horror at Valcarm's crimes. He would shake his head, and swing his whole body, and blow out the breath from behind his cheeks, knitting his eyebrows and assuming a look of terror when it was suggested to him that the daughter of his old friend, the undoubted owner of a house in Nuremberg, was anxious to give herself and her property to Ludovic Valcarm. 'No, no, Madame Staubach, that mustn't be; —that must not be, my dear Madame. A rebel! a traitor! I don't know what the young man hasn't done. It would be confiscated;—confiscated! Dear, dear, only to think of Josef Tressel's daughter! Let her marry Peter Steinmarc, a good man,—a very good man! Followed her father, you know, and does his work very well. The city is not what it used to be, Madame Staubach, but still Peter does his work very well.' Then Herr Molk promised to come down to the red house, and he did come down.

But Madame Staubach could not trust everything to Herr Molk. It was necessary that she should do much before he came, and much probably after he went. As her conception of the true state of things became strong,

and as she was convinced also that Linda was really far
from well, her manner became kinder, and she assumed
that sickbed tenderness which admitted of sleep during
the reading of a sermon. But it was essential that she
should not forget her work for an hour. Gradually Linda
was taught to understand that on such a day Steinmarc
was to demand an answer. When Linda attempted to
explain that the answer had been already given, and could
not be altered, her aunt interrupted her, declaring that
nothing need be said at the present moment. So that the
question remained an open question, and Linda understood that it was so regarded. Then Madame Staubach
spoke of Ludovic Valcarm, putting up her hands with
dismay, and declaring what horrid things Herr Molk had
told of him. It was at that moment that Linda was told
that she was to be visited in a day or two by the burgomaster. Linda endeavoured to explain that though it
might be necessary to give up Ludovic,—not saying that
she would give him up,—still it was not on that account
necessary also that she should marry Peter Steinmarc.
Madame Staubach shook her head, and implied that the
necessity did exist. Things had been said, and things
had been done, and Herr Molk was decidedly of opinion
that the marriage should be solemnised without delay.
Linda, of course, did not submit to this in silence; but
gradually she became more and more silent as her aunt
continued in a low tone to drone forth her wishes and her
convictions, and at last Linda would almost sleep while
the salutary position of Peter Steinmarc's wife was being
explained to her.

The reader must understand that she was in truth ill,
prostrated by misery, doubt, and agitation, and weak
from the effects of her illness. In this condition Herr Molk
paid his visit to her. He spoke, in the first place, of the
civil honour which she had inherited from her respected
father, and of all that she owed to Nuremberg on this
account. Then he spoke also of that other inheritance,
the red house, explaining to her that it was her duty as
a citizen to see that this should not be placèd by her in
evil hands. After that he took up the subject of Peter

Steinmarc's merits; and according to Herr Molk, as he now drew the picture, Peter was little short of a municipal demigod. Prudent he was, and confidential. A man deep in the city's trust, and with money laid out at interest. Strong and healthy he was,—indeed lusty for his age, if Herr Molk spoke the truth. Poor Linda gave a little kick beneath the clothes when this was said, but she spoke no word of reply. And then Peter was a man not given to scolding, of equal temper, who knew his place, and would not interfere with things that did not belong to him. Herr Molk produced a catalogue of nuptial virtues, and endowed Peter with them all. When this was completed, he came to the last head of his discourse,—the last head and the most important. Ludovic Valcarm was still in prison, and there was no knowing what might be done to him. To be imprisoned for life in some horrible place among the rats seemed to be the least of it. Linda, when she heard this, gave one slight scream, but she said nothing. Because Herr Molk was a burgomaster, she need not on that account believe every word that fell from his mouth. But the cruellest blow of all was at the end. When Ludovic was taken, there had been—a young woman with him.

'What young woman?' said Linda, turning sharply upon the burgomaster.

'Not such a young woman as any young man ought to be seen with,' said Herr Molk.

'What matters her name?' said Madame Staubach, who, during the whole discourse, had been sitting silent by the bedside.

'I don't believe a word of it,' said Linda.

'I saw the young woman in his company, my dear. She had a felt hat and a blue frock. But, my child, you know nothing of the lives of such young men as this. It would not astonish me if he knew a dozen young women! You don't suppose that such a one as he ever means to be true?'

'I am sure he meant to be true to me,' said Linda.

'T-sh, t-sh, t-sh! my dear child; you don't know the world, and how should you? If you want to marry a husband who will remain at home and live discreetly, and be true to you, you must take such a man as Peter Steinmarc.

'Of course she must,' said Madame Staubach.

'Such a one as Ludovic Valcarm would only waste your property and drag you into the gutters.'

'No more—no more,' said Madame Staubach.

'She will think better of it, Madame Staubach. She will not be so foolish nor so wicked as that,' said the burgomaster.

'May the Lord in His mercy give her light to see the right way,' said Madame Staubach.

Then Herr Molk took his departure with Madame Staubach at his heels, and Linda was left to her own considerations. Her first assertion to herself was that she did not believe a word of it. She knew what sort of a man she could love as her husband without having Herr Molk to come and teach her. She could not love Peter Steinmarc, let him be ever so much respected in Nuremberg. As to what Herr Molk said that she owed to the city, that was nothing to her. The city did not care for her, nor she for the city. If they wished to take the house from her, let them do it. She was quite sure that Ludovic Valcarm had not loved her because she was the owner of a paltry old house. As to Ludovic being in prison, the deeper was his dungeon, the more true it behoved her to be to him. If he were among the rats, she would willingly be there also. But when she tried to settle in her thoughts the matter of the young woman with the felt hat and the blue frock, then her mind became more doubtful.

She knew well enough that Herr Molk was wrong in the picture which he drew of Peter; but she was not so sure that he was wrong in that other picture about Ludovic. There was something very grand, that had gratified her spirit amazingly, in the manner in which her lover had disappeared among the rafters; but at the same time she acknowledged to herself that there was much in it that was dangerous. A young man who can disappear among the rafters so quickly must have had much experience. She knew that Ludovic was wild,—

very wild, and that wild young men do not make good
husbands. To have had his arm once round her waist
was to her almost a joy for ever. But she had nearly come
to believe that if she were to have his arm often round
her waist, she must become a castaway. And then, to be
a castaway, sharing her treasure with another! Who was
this blue-frocked woman, with a felt hat, who seemed to
have been willing to do so much more for Ludovic than
she had done,—who had gone with him into danger, and
was sharing with him his perils?

But though she made a great fight against the wisdom
of Herr Molk when she was first left to herself, the words
of the burgomaster had their effect. Her enemies were
becoming too strong for her. Her heart was weak within
her. She had eaten little or nothing for the last few days,
and the blood was running thinly through her veins.
It was more difficult to reply to tenderness from her aunt
than to harshness. And there came upon her a feeling
that after all it signified but little. There was but a
choice between one misery and another. The only really
good thing would be to die and to have done with it all,
—to die before she had utterly thrown away all hope, all
chance of happiness in that future world in which she
thoroughly believed. She was ill now, and if it might be
that her illness would bring her to death;—but would
bring her slowly, so that she might yet repent, and all
would be right.

Madame Staubach said nothing more to her about
Peter till the morning of that day on which Peter was to
come for his answer. A little before noon Madame
Staubach brought to her niece some weak broth, as she
had done once before, on that morning. But Linda, who
was sick and faint at heart, would not take it.

'Try, my dear,' said Madame Staubach.

'I cannot try,' said Linda.

'I wish particularly to speak to you,—now,—at once;
and this will give you strength to listen to me.' But
Linda declined to be made strong for such a purpose, and
declared that she could listen very well as she was. Then
Madame Staubach began her great argument. Linda

had heard what the burgomaster had said. Linda knew
well what she, her aunt and guardian, thought about it.
Linda could not but know that visits from a young man
at her chamber door, such as that to which she herself
had confessed, were things so horrible that they hardly
admitted of being spoken of even between an aunt and
her niece; and Madame Staubach's cheeks were hot and
red as she spoke of this.

'If he had come to your door, aunt Charlotte, you
could not have helped it.'

'But he embraced you?'

'Yes, he did.'

'Oh, my child, will you not let me save you from the
evil days? Linda, you are all in all to me;—the only one
that I love. Linda, Linda, your soul is precious to me,
almost as my own. Oh, Linda, shall I pray for you in
vain?' She sank upon her knees as she spoke, and prayed
with all her might that God would turn the heart of
this child, so that even yet she might be rescued from
the burning. With arms extended, and loud voice, and
dishevelled hair, and streaming tears, shrieking to Heaven
in her agony, every now and again kissing the hand of
the poor sinner, she besought the Lord her God that He
would give to her the thing for which she asked;—and
that thing prayed for with such agony of earnestness, was
a consent from Linda to marry Peter Steinmarc! It was
very strange, but the woman was as sincere in her prayer
as is faith itself. She would have cut herself with knives,
and have swallowed ashes whole, could she have believed
that by doing so she could have been nearer her object.
And she had no end of her own in view. That Peter, as
master of the house, would be a thorn in her own side,
she had learned to believe; but thorns in the sides of
women were, she thought, good for them; and it was
necessary to Linda that she should be stuck full of thorns,
so that her base human desires might, as it were, fall from
her bones and perish out of the way. Once, twice, thrice,
Linda besought her aunt to arise; but the half frantic
woman had said to herself that she would remain on her
knees, on the hard boards, till this thing was granted to

her. Had it not been said by lips that could not lie, that faith would move a mountain? and would not faith, real faith, do for her this smaller thing? Then there came questions to her mind, whether the faith was there. Did she really believe that this thing would be done for her? If she believed it, then it would be done. Thinking of all this, with the girl's hands between her own, she renewed her prayers. Once and again she threw herself upon the floor, striking it with her forehead. 'Oh, my child! my child, my child! If God would do this for me! my child, my child! Only for my sin and weakness this thing would be done for me.'

For three hours Linda lay there, hearing this, mingling her screams with those of her aunt, half fainting, half dead, now and again dozing for a moment even amidst the screams, and then struggling up in bed, that she might embrace her aunt, and implore her to abandon her purpose. But the woman would only give herself with the greater vehemence to the work. 'Now, if the Lord would see fit, now,—now; if the Lord would see fit!'

Linda had swooned, her aunt being all unconscious of it, had dozed afterwards, and had then risen and struggled up, and was seated in her bed. 'Aunt Charlotte,' she said, 'what is it—that—you want of me?'

'That you should obey the Lord, and take this man for your husband.'

Linda stayed a while to think, not pausing that she might answer her aunt's sophistry, which she hardly noticed, but that she might consider, if it were possible, what it was that she was about to do;—that there might be left a moment to her before she had surrendered herself for ever to her doom. And then she spoke. 'Aunt Charlotte,' she said, 'if you will get up I will do as you would have me.'

Madame Staubach could not arise at once, as it was incumbent on her to return thanks for the mercy that had been vouchsafed to her; but her thanks were quickly rendered, and then she was on the bed, with Linda in her arms. She had succeeded, and her child was saved. Perhaps there was something of triumph that the earnestness of her prayer should have been efficacious. It was a great thing that she had done, and the Scriptures had proved themselves to be true to her. She lay for a while fondling her niece and kissing her, as she had not done for years. 'Linda, dear Linda!' She almost promised to the girl earthly happiness, in spite of her creed as to the necessity for crushing. For the moment she petted her niece as one weak woman may pet another. She went down to the kitchen and made coffee for her,—though she herself was weak from want of food,—and toasted bread, and brought the food up with a china cup and a china plate, to show her gratitude to the niece who had been her convert. And yet, as she did so, she told herself that such gratitude was mean, vile, and mistaken. It had been the Lord's doing, and not Linda's.

Linda took the coffee and the toast, and tried to make herself passive in her aunt's hands. She returned Madame Staubach's kisses and the pressure of her hand, and made some semblance of joy, that peace should have been re-established between them two. But her heart was dead within her, and the reflection that this illness might even yet be an illness unto death was the only one in which she could find the slightest comfort. She had promised Ludovic that she would never become the wife of any one but him; and now, at the first trial of her faith, she had promised to marry Peter Steinmarc. She was forsworn, and it would hardly be that the Lord would be satisfied with her, because she had perjured herself! When her aunt left her, which Madame Staubach did as the dusk came on, she endeavoured to promise herself that she would never get well. Was not the very thought that she would have to take Peter for her husband enough to keep her on her sickbed till she should be beyond all such perils as that?

Madame Staubach, before she left the room, asked Linda whether she would not be able to dress herself and come down, so that she might say one word to her affianced husband. It should be but one word, and then she should be allowed to return. Linda would have declined to do this,—was refusing utterly to do it,—

when she found that if she did not go down Peter would
be brought up to her bedroom, to receive her troth there,
by her bedside. The former evil, she thought, would be
less than the latter. Steinmarc as a lover at her bedside
would be intolerable to her; and then if she descended,
she might ascend again instantly. That was part of the
bargain. But if Peter were to come up to her room, there
was no knowing how long he might stay there. She promised therefore that she would dress and come down as
soon as she knew that the man was in the parlour. We
may say for her, that when left alone she was as firmly
resolved as ever that she would never become the man's
wife. If this illness did not kill her, she would escape from
the wedding in some other way. She would never put
her hand into that of Peter Steinmarc, and let the priest
call him and her man and wife. She had lied to her aunt
—so she told herself,—but her aunt had forced the lie
from her.

When Peter entered Madame Staubach's parlour he
was again dressed in his Sunday best, as he had been
when he made his first overture to Linda. 'Good evening,
Madame Staubach,' he said.

'Good evening, Peter Steinmarc.'

'I hope you have good news for me, Madame Staubach,
from the maiden up-stairs.'

Madame Staubach took a moment or two for thought
before she replied. 'Peter Steinmarc, the Lord has been
good to us, and has softened her heart, and has brought
the child round to our way of thinking. She has consented, Peter, that you should be her husband.'

Peter was not so grateful perhaps as he should have
been at this good news,—or rather perhaps at the manner
in which the result seemed to have been achieved. Of
course he knew nothing of those terribly earnest petitions
which Madame Staubach had preferred to the throne of
heaven on behalf of his marriage, but he did not like
being told at all of any interposition from above in such
a matter. He would have preferred to be assured, even
though he himself might not quite have believed the
assurance, that Linda had yielded to a sense of his own

merits. 'I am glad she has thought better of it, Madame
Staubach,' he said; 'she is only just in time.'

Madame Staubach was very nearly angry, but she
reminded herself that people cannot be crushed by rose-
leaves. Peter Steinmarc was to be taken, because he was
Peter Steinmarc, not because he was somebody very
different, better mannered, and more agreeable.

'I don't know how that may be, Peter.'

'Ah, but it is so;—only just in time, I can assure you.
But "a miss is as good as a mile;" so we will let that pass.'

'She is now ready to come down and accept your troth,
and give you hers. You will remember that she is ill and
weak; and, indeed, I am unwell myself. She can stay
but a moment, and then, I am sure, you will leave us for
to-night. The day has not been without its trouble and
its toil to both of us.'

'Surely,' said Peter; 'a word or two shall satisfy me
to-night. But, Madame Staubach, I shall look to you to
see that the period before our wedding is not protracted,
—you will remember that.' To this Madame Staubach
made no answer, but slowly mounted to Linda's chamber.

Linda was already nearly dressed. She was not
minded to keep her suitor waiting. Tetchen was with
her, aiding her; but to Tetchen she had refused to say a
single word respecting either Peter or Ludovic. Something Tetchen had heard from Madame Staubach, but
from Linda she heard nothing. Linda intended to go
down to the parlour, and therefore she must dress herself.
As she was weak almost to fainting, she had allowed
Tetchen to help her. Her aunt led her down, and there
was nothing said between them as they went. At the
door her aunt kissed her, and muttered some word of
love. Then they entered the room together.

Peter was found standing in the middle of the chamber,
with his left hand beneath his waistcoat, and his right
hand free for the performance of some graceful salutation.
'Linda,' said he, as soon as he saw the two ladies standing
a few feet away from him, 'I am glad to see you down-
stairs again,—very glad. I hope you find yourself better.'
Linda muttered, or tried to mutter, some words of thanks;

but nothing was audible. She stood hanging upon her aunt, with eyes turned down, and her limbs trembling beneath her. 'Linda,' continued Peter, 'your aunt tells me that you have accepted my offer. I am very glad of it. I will be a good husband to you, and I hope you will be an obedient wife.'

'Linda,' said Madame Staubach, 'put your hand in his.' Linda put forth her little hand a few inches, and Peter took it within his own, looking the while into Madame Staubach's face, as though he were to repeat some form of words after her. 'You are now betrothed in the sight of God, as man and wife,' said Madame Staubach; 'and may the married life of both of you be passed to His glory.—Amen.'

'Amen,' said Steinmarc, like the parish clerk. Linda pressed her lips close together, so that there should be no possibility of a chance sound passing from them.

'Now, I think we will go back again, Peter, as the poor child can hardly stand.' Peter raised no objection, and then Linda was conducted back again to her bed. There was one comfort to her in the remembrance of the scene. She had escaped the dreaded contamination of a kiss.

CHAPTER X

PETER STEINMARC, now that he was an engaged man, affianced to a young bride, was urgent from day to day with Madame Staubach that the date of his wedding should be fixed. He soon found that all Nuremberg knew that he was to be married. Perhaps Herr Molk had not been so silent and discreet as would have been becoming in a man so highly placed, and perhaps Peter himself had let slip a word to some confidential friend who had betrayed him. Be this as it might, all Nuremberg knew of Peter's good fortune, and he soon found that he should have no peace till the thing was completed. 'She is quite well enough, I am sure,' said Peter to Madame Staubach, 'and if there is anything amiss she can finish getting well afterwards.' Madame Staubach was sufficiently eager herself that Linda should be married

without delay; but, nevertheless, she was angry at being
so pressed, and used rather sharp language in explaining
to Peter that he would not be allowed to dictate on such
a subject. 'Ah! well; if it isn't this year it won't be next,'
said Peter, on one occasion when he had determined to
show his power. Madame Staubach did not believe the
threat, but she did begin to fear that, perhaps, after all,
there might be fresh obstacles. It was now near the end
of November, and though Linda still kept her room, her
aunt could not see that she was suffering from any real
illness. When, however, a word was said to press the
poor girl, Linda would declare that she was weak and
sick—unable to walk; in short, that at present she would
not leave her room. Madame Staubach was beginning
to be angered at this; but, for all that, Linda had not left
her room.

It was now two weeks since she had suffered herself
to be betrothed, and Peter had twice been up to her
chamber, creaking with his shoes along the passages.
Twice she had passed a terrible half-hour, while he had
sat, for the most part silent, in an old wicker chair by her
bedside. Her aunt had, of course, been present, and had
spoken most of the words that had been uttered during
these visits; and these words had nearly altogether
referred to Linda's ailments. Linda was still not quite
well, she had said, but would soon be better, and then all
would be properly settled. Such was the purport of the
words which Madame Staubach would speak on those
occasions.

'Before Christmas?' Peter had once asked.

'No,' Linda had replied, very sharply.

'It must be as the Lord shall will it,' said Madame
Staubach. That had been so true that neither Linda nor
Peter had found it necessary to express dissent. On both
these occasions Linda's energy had been chiefly used to
guard herself from any sign of a caress. Peter had
thought of it, but Linda lay far away upon the bed, and
the lover did not see how it was to be managed. He was
not sure, moreover, whether Madame Staubach would
not have been shocked at any proposal in reference to

an antenuptial embrace. On these considerations he abstained.

It was now near the end of November, and Linda knew that she was well. Her aunt had proposed some day in January for the marriage, and Linda, though she had never assented, could not on the moment find any plea for refusing altogether to have a day fixed. All she could do was to endeavour to stave off the evil. Madame Staubach seemed to think that it was indispensable that a day in January should be named; therefore, at last, the thirtieth of that month was after some fashion fixed for the wedding. Linda never actually assented, but after many discourses it seemed to be decided that it should be so. Peter was so told, and with some grumbling expressed himself as satisfied; but when would Linda come down to him? He was sure that Linda was well enough to come down if she would. At last a day was fixed for that also. It was arranged that the three should go to church together on the first Sunday in December. It would be safer so than in any other way. He could not make love to her in church.

On the Saturday evening Linda was down-stairs with her aunt. Peter, as she knew well, was at the Rothe Ross on that evening, and would not be home till past ten. Tetchen was out, and Linda had gone down to take her supper with her aunt. The meal had been eaten almost in silence, for Linda was very sad, and Madame Staubach herself was beginning to feel that the task before her was almost too much for her strength. Had it not been that she was carried on by the conviction that things stern and hard and cruel would in the long-run be comforting to the soul, she would have given way. But she was a woman not prone to give way when she thought that the soul's welfare was concerned. She had seen the shrinking, retreating horror with which Linda had almost involuntarily contrived to keep her distance from her future husband. She had listened to the girl's voice, and knew that there had been no one light-hearted tone from it since that consent had been wrung from the sufferer by the vehemence of her own bedside prayers. She was aware that Linda from day to day was becoming thinner and thinner, paler and still paler. But she knew, or thought that she knew, that it was God's will; and so she went on. It was not a happy time even for Madame Staubach, but it was a time in which to Linda it seemed that hell had come to her beforehand with all its terrors.

There was, however, one thing certain to her yet. She would never put her hand into that of Peter Steinmarc in God's house after such a fashion that any priest should be able to say that they two were man and wife in the sight of God.

On this Saturday evening Tetchen was out, as was the habit with her on alternate Saturday evenings. On such occasions Linda would usually do what household work was necessary in the kitchen, preparatory to the coming Sabbath. But on this evening Madame Staubach herself was employed in the kitchen, as Linda was not considered to be well enough to perform the task. Linda was sitting alone, between the fire and the window, with no work in her hand, with no book before her, thinking of her fate, when there came upon the panes of the window sundry small, sharp, quickly-repeated rappings, as though gravel had been thrown upon them. She knew at once that the noise was not accidental, and jumped up on her feet. If it was some mode of escape, let it be what it might, she would accept it. She jumped up, and with short hurried steps placed herself close to the window. The quick, sharp, little blows upon the glass were heard again, and then there was a voice. 'Linda, Linda.' Heavens and earth! it was his voice. There was no mistaking it. Had she heard but a single syllable in the faintest whisper, she would have known it. It was Ludovic Valcarm, and he had come for her, even out of his prison. He should find that he had not come in vain. Then the word was repeated—'Linda, are you there?' 'I am here,' she said, speaking very faintly, and trembling at the sound of her own voice. Then the iron pin was withdrawn from the wooden shutter on the outside, as it could not have been withdrawn had not some traitor within the house prepared the way for it, and the heavy Venetian blinds were folded back, and Linda could see the outlines of the man's head and shoulders, in the dark, close to the panes of the window. It was raining at the time, and the night was very dark, but still she could see the outline. She stood and watched him; for, though she was willing to be with him, she felt that she could do nothing. In a moment the frame of the window was raised, and his head was within the room, within her aunt's parlour, where her aunt might now have been for all that he could have known; —were it not that Tetchen was watching at the corner, and knew to the scraping of a carrot how long it would be before Madame Staubach had made the soup for to-morrow's dinner.

'Linda,' he said, 'how is it with you?'

'Oh, Ludovic!'

'Linda, will you go with me now?'

'What! now, this instant?'

'To-night. Listen, dearest, for she will be back. Go to her in ten minutes from now, and tell her that you are weary and would be in bed. She will see you to your room perhaps, and there may be delay. But when you can, come down silently, with your thickest cloak and your strongest hat, and any little thing you can carry easily. Come without a candle, and creep to the passage window. I will be there. If she will let you go up-stairs alone, you may be there in half-an-hour. It is our only chance.' Then the window was closed, and after that the shutter, and then the pin was pushed back, and Linda was again alone in her aunt's chamber.

To be there in half-an-hour! To commence such a job as this at once! To go to her aunt with a premeditated lie that would require perfect acting, and to have to do this in ten minutes, in five minutes, while the minutes were flying from her like sparks of fire! It was impossible. If it had been enjoined upon her for the morrow, so that there should have been time for thought, she might have done it. But this call upon her for instant action almost paralysed her. And yet what other hope was there? She had told herself that she would do anything, however wicked, however dreadful, that would save her from the

proposed marriage. She had sworn to herself that she
would do something; for that Steinmarc's wife she would
never be. And here had come to her a possibility of
escape,—of escape too which had in it so much of sweetness! She must lie to her aunt. Was not every hour of
life a separate lie? And as for acting a lie, what was the
difference between that and telling it, except in the
capability of the liar. Her aunt had forced her to lie. No
truth was any longer possible to her. Would it not be
better to lie for Ludovic Valcarm than to lie for Peter
Steinmarc? She looked at the upright clock which stood
in the corner of the room, and, seeing that the ten
minutes was already passed, she crossed at once over into
the kitchen. Her aunt was standing there, and Tetchen
with her bonnet on, was standing by. Tetchen, as soon
as she saw Linda, explained that she must be off again
at once. She had only returned to fetch some article
for a little niece of hers which Madame Staubach had
given her.

'Aunt Charlotte,' said Linda, 'I am very weary. You
will not be angry, will you, if I go to bed?'

'It is not yet nine o'clock, my dear.'

'But I am tired, and I fear that I shall lack strength
for to-morrow.' Oh, Linda, Linda! But, indeed, had
you foreseen the future, you might have truly said that
you would want strength on the morrow.

'Then go, my dear;' and Madame Staubach kissed her
niece and blessed her, and after that, with careful hand,
threw some salt into the pot that was simmering on the
stove. Peter Steinmarc was to dine with them on the
morrow, and he was a man who cared that his soup
should be well seasoned. Linda, terribly smitten by the
consciousness of her own duplicity, went forth, and crept
up-stairs to her room. She had now, as she calculated, a
quarter of an hour, and she would wish, if possible, to be
punctual. She looked out for a moment from the window,
and could only see that it was very dark, and could hear
that it was raining hard. She took her thickest cloak and
her strongest hat. She would do in all things as he bade
her; and then she tried to think what else she would take.

She was going forth,—whither she knew not. Then came
upon her a thought that on the morrow,—for many
morrows afterwards, perhaps for all morrows to come,
—there would be no comfortable wardrobe to which
she could go for such decent changes of raiment as
she required. She looked at her frock, and having one
darker and thicker than that she wore, she changed it
instantly. And then it was not only her garments
that she was leaving behind her. For ever afterwards,
—for ever and ever and ever,—she must be a castaway.
The die had been thrown now, and everything was
over. She was leaving behind her all decency, all
feminine respect, all the clean ways of her pure young
life, all modest thoughts, all honest, serviceable daily
tasks, all godliness, all hope of heaven! The silent, quick-
running tears streamed down her face as she moved
rapidly about the room. The thing must be done, must
be done,—must be done, even though earth and heaven
were to fail her for ever afterwards. Earth and heaven
would fail her for ever afterwards, but still the thing
must be done. All should be endured, if by that all she
could escape from the man she loathed.

She collected a few things, what little store of money
she had,—four or five gulden, perhaps,—and a pair of light
shoes and clean stockings, and a fresh handkerchief or
two, and a little collar, and then she started. He had told
her to bring what she could carry easily. She must not
disobey him, but she would fain have brought more had
she dared. At the last moment she returned, and took a
small hair-brush and a comb. Then she looked round
the room with a hurried glance, put out her candle, and
crept silently down the stairs. On the first landing she
paused, for it was possible that Peter might be returning.
She listened, and then remembered that she would have
heard Peter's feet even on the walk outside. Very
quickly, but still more gently than ever, she went down
the last stairs. From the foot of the stairs into the passage
there was a moment in which she must be within sight
of the kitchen door. She flew by, and felt that she must
have been seen. But she was not seen. In an instant she

was at the open window, and in another instant she was standing beside her lover on the gravel path. What he said to her she did not hear; what he did she did not know. She had completed her task now; she had done her part, and had committed herself entirely into his hands. She would ask no question. She would trust him entirely. She only knew that at the moment his arm was round her, and that she was being lifted off the bank into the river.

'Dearest girl! can you see? No; nothing, of course, as yet. Step down. There is a boat here. There are two boats. Lean upon me, and we can walk over. There. Do not mind treading softly. They cannot hear because of the rain. We shall be out of it in a minute. I am sorry you should be wet, but yet it is better for us.'

She hardly understood him, but yet she did as he told her, and in a few minutes she was standing on the other bank of the river, in the Ruden Platz. Here Linda perceived that there was a man awaiting them, to whom Ludovic gave certain orders about the boats. Then Ludovic took her by the hand and ran with her across the Platz, till they stood beneath the archway of the brewery warehouse where she had so often watched him as he went in and out. 'Here we are safe,' he said, stooping down and kissing her, and brushing away the drops of rain from the edges of her hair. Oh, what safety! To be there, in the middle of the night, with him, and not know whither she was to go, where she was to lie, whether she would ever again know that feeling of security which had been given to her throughout her whole life by her aunt's presence and the walls of her own house. Safe! Was ever peril equal to hers? 'Linda, say that you love me. Say that you are my own.'

'I do love you,' she said; 'otherwise how should I be here?'

'And you had promised to marry that man!'

'I should never have married him. I should have died.'

'Dearest Linda! But come; you must not stand here.' Then he took her up, up the warehouse stairs into a gloomy chamber, from which there was a window looking on to the Ruden Platz, and there, with many caresses, he explained to her his plans. The caresses she endeavoured to avoid, and, when she could not avoid them, to moderate. 'Would he remember,' she asked, 'just for the present, all that she had gone through, and spare her for a while, because she was so weak?' She made her little appeal with swimming eyes and low voice, looking into his face, holding his great hand the while between her own. He swore that she was his queen, and should have her way in everything. But would she not give him one kiss? He reminded her that she had never kissed him. She did as he asked her, just touching his lips with hers, and then she stood by him, leaning on him, while he explained to her something of his plans. He kept close to the window, as it was necessary that he should keep his eyes upon the red house.

His plan was this. There was a train which passed by the Nuremberg station on its way to Augsburg at three o'clock in the morning. By this train he proposed that they should travel to that city. He had, he said, the means of providing accommodation for her there, and no one would know whither they had gone. He did not anticipate that any one in the house opposite would learn that Linda had escaped till the next morning; but should any suspicion have been aroused, and should the fact be ascertained, there would certainly be lights moving in the house, and light would be seen from the window of Linda's own chamber. Therefore he proposed, during the long hours that they must yet wait, to stand in his present spot and watch, so that he might know at the first moment whether there was any commotion among the inmates of the red house. 'There goes old Peter to bed,' said he; 'he won't be the first to find out, I'll bet a florin.' And afterwards he signified the fact that Madame Staubach had gone to her chamber. This was the moment of danger, as it might be very possible that Madame Staubach would go into Linda's room. In that case, as he said, he had a little carriage outside the walls which would take them to the first town on the route to Augsburg. Had a light been seen but for

a moment in Linda's room they were to start; and would
certainly reach the spot where the carriage stood before
any followers could be on their heels. But Madame
Staubach went to her own room without noticing that of
her niece, and then the red house was all dark and all
still. They would have made the best of their way to
Augsburg before their flight would be discovered.

During the minutes in which they were watching the
lights Linda stood close to her lover, leaning on his
shoulder, and supported by his arm. But this was over by
ten, and then there remained nearly five hours, during
which they must stay in their present hiding-place. Up
to this time Linda's strength had supported her under
the excitement of her escape, but now she was like to
faint, and it was necessary at any rate that she should be
allowed to lie down. He got sacks for her from some part
of the building, and with these constructed for her a bed
on the floor, near to the spot which he must occupy himself in still keeping his eye upon the red house. He laid
her down and covered her feet with sacking, and put
sacks under her head for a pillow. He was very gentle
with her, and she thanked him over and over again, and
endeavoured to think that her escape had been fortunate,
and that her position was happy. Had she not succeeded
in flying from Peter Steinmarc? And after such a flight
would not all idea of a marriage with him be out of the
question? For some little time she was cheered by talking
to him. She asked him about his imprisonment. 'Ah!'
said he; 'if I cannot be one too many for such an old
fogey as Herr Molk, I'll let out my brains to an ass, and
take to grazing on thistles.' His offence had been political, and had been committed in conjunction with others.
And he and they were sure of success ultimately,—were
sure of success very speedily. Linda could understand
nothing of the subject. But she could hope that her lover
might prosper in his undertaking, and she could admire
and love him for encountering the dangers of such an
enterprise. And then, half sportively, half in earnest, she
taxed him with that matter which was next her heart.
Who had been the young woman with the blue frock and

the felt hat who had been with him when he was brought before the magistrates?

'Young woman;——with blue frock! who told you of the young woman, Linda?' He came and knelt beside her as he asked the question, leaving his watch for the moment; and she could see by the dim light of the lamp outside that there was a smile upon his face,—almost joyous, full of mirth.

'Who told me? The magistrate you were taken to; Herr Molk told me himself,' said Linda, almost happily. That smile upon his face had in some way vanquished her feeling of jealousy.

'Then he is a greater scoundrel than I took him to be, or else a more utter fool. The girl in the blue frock, Linda, was one of our young men, who was to get out of the city in that disguise. And I believe Herr Molk knew it when he tried to set you against me, by telling you the story.'

Whether Herr Molk had known this, or whether he had simply been fool enough to be taken in by the blue frock and the felt hat, it is not for us to inquire here. But Ludovic was greatly amused at the story, and Linda was charmed at the explanation she had received. It was only an extra feather in her lover's cap that he should have been connected with a blue frock and felt hat under such circumstances as those now explained to her. Then he went back to the window, and she turned on her side and attempted to sleep.

To be in all respects a castaway,—a woman to whom other women would not speak! She knew that such was her position now. She had done a deed which would separate her for ever from those who were respectable, and decent, and good. Peter Steinmarc would utterly despise her. It was very well that something should have occurred which would make it impossible that he should any longer wish to marry her; but it would be very bitter to her to be rejected even by him because she was unfit to be an honest man's wife. And then she asked herself questions about her young lover, who was so handsome, so bold, so tender to her; who was in all outward respects

just what a lover should be. Would he wish to marry her
after she had thus consented to fly with him, alone, at
night: or would he wish that she should be his light-of-
love, as her aunt had been once cruel enough to call her?
There would be no cruelty, at any rate no injustice, in so
calling her now. And should there be any hesitation on
his part, would she ask him to make her his wife? It was
very terrible to her to think that it might come to pass
that she should have on her knees to implore this man to
marry her. He had called her his queen, but he had
never said that she should be his wife. And would any
pastor marry them, coming to him, as they must come,
as two runaways? She knew that certain preliminaries
were necessary,—certain bidding of banns, and processes
before the magistrates. Her own banns and those of her
betrothed, Peter Steinmarc, had been asked once in the
church of St. Lawrence, as she had heard with infinite
disgust. She did not see that it was possible that Ludovic
should marry her, even if he were willing to do so. But
it was too late to think of all this now; and she could only
moisten the rough sacking with her tears.

'You had better get up now, dearest,' said Ludovic,
again bending over her.

'Has the time come?'

'Yes; the time has come, and we must be moving. The
rain is over, which is a comfort. It is as dark as pitch,
too. Cling close to me. I should know my way if I were
blindfold.'

She did cling close to him, and he conducted her
through narrow streets and passages out to the city gate,
which led to the railway station. Nuremberg has still
gates like a fortified town, and there are, I believe,
porters at the gates with huge keys. Nuremberg delights
to perpetuate the memories of things that are gone. But
ingress and egress are free to everybody, by night as well
as by day, as it must be when railway trains arrive and
start at three in the morning; and the burgomaster and
warders, and sentinels and porters, though they still
carry the keys, know that the glory of their house has
gone.

Railway tickets for two were given to Linda without a question,—for to her was intrusted the duty of procuring them,—and they were soon hurrying away towards Augsburg through the dark night. At any rate they had been successful in escaping. 'After to-morrow we will be as happy as the day is long,' said Ludovic, as he pressed his companion close to his side. Linda told herself, but did not tell him, that she never could be happy again.

CHAPTER XI

THEY were whirled away through the dark cold night with the noise of the rattling train ever in their ears. Though there had been a railway running close by Nuremberg now for many years, Linda was not herself so well accustomed to travelling as will probably be most of those who will read this tale of her sufferings. Now and again in the day-time, and generally in fair weather, she had gone as far as Fürth, and on one occasion even as far as Würzburg with her aunt when there had been a great gathering of German Anabaptists at that town; but she had never before travelled at night, and she had certainly never before travelled in such circumstances as those which now enveloped her. When she entered the carriage, she was glad to see that there were other persons present. There was a woman, though the woman was so closely muffled and so fast asleep that Linda, throughout the whole morning, did not know whether her fellow-traveller was young or old. Nevertheless, the presence of the woman was in some sort a comfort to her, and there were two men in the carriage, and a little boy. She hardly understood why, but she felt that it was better for her to have fellow-travellers. Neither of them, however, spoke above a word or two either to her or to her lover. At first she sat at a little distance from Ludovic,— or rather induced him to allow that there should be some space between them; but gradually she suffered him to come closer to her, and she dozed with her head upon his shoulder. Very little was said between them. He

whispered to her from time to time sundry little words
of love, calling her his queen, his own one, his life, and the
joy of his eyes. But he told her little or nothing of his
future plans, as she would have wished that he should
do. She asked him, however, no questions;—none at
least till their journey was nearly over. The more that
his conduct warranted her want of trust, the more
unwilling did she become to express any diffidence or
suspicion.

After a while she became very cold;—so cold that that
now became for the moment her greatest cause of suffering. It was mid-winter, and though the cloak she had
brought was the warmest garment that she possessed, it
was very insufficient for such work as the present night
had brought upon her. Besides her cloak, she had nothing
wherewith to wrap herself. Her feet became like ice, and
then the chill crept up her body; and though she clung
very close to her lover, she could not keep herself from
shivering as though in an ague fit. She had no hesitation
now in striving to obtain some warmth by his close
proximity. It seemed to her as though the cold would
kill her before she could reach Augsburg. The train
would not be due there till nine in the morning, and it
was still dark night as she thought that it would be
impossible for her to sustain such an agony of pain much
longer. It was still dark night, and the violent rain was
pattering against the glass, and the damp came in
through the crevices, and the wind blew bitterly upon
her; and then as she turned a little to ask her lover to find
some comfort for her, some mitigation of her pain, she
perceived that he was asleep. Then the tears began to
run down her cheeks, and she told herself that it would
be well if she could die.

After all, what did she know of this man who was now
sleeping by her side,—this man to whom she had intrusted
everything, more than her happiness, her very soul?
How many words had she ever spoken to him? What
assurance had she even of his heart? Why was he asleep,
while her sufferings were so very cruel to her? She had
encountered the evils of this elopement to escape what

had appeared to her the greater evils of a detested
marriage. Steinmarc was very much to be hated. But
might it not be that even that would have been better
than this? Poor girl! the illusion even of her love was
being frozen cold within her during the agony of that
morning. All the while the train went thundering on
through the night, now rushing into a tunnel, now cross-
ing a river, and at every change in the sounds of the
carriages she almost hoped that something might be
amiss. Oh, the cold! She had gathered her feet up and
was trying to sit on them. For a moment or two she had
hoped that her movement would waken Ludovic, so that
she might have had the comfort of a word; but he had
only tumbled with his head hither and thither, and had
finally settled himself in a position in which he leaned
heavily upon her. She thought that he was heartless to
sleep while she was suffering; but she forgot that he had
watched at the window while she had slumbered upon
the sacks in the warehouse. At length, however, she
could bear his weight no longer, and she was forced to
rouse him. 'You are so heavy,' she said; 'I cannot bear
it;' when at last she succeeded in inducing him to sit
upright.

'Dear me! oh, ah, yes. How cold it is! I think I have
been asleep.'

'The cold is killing me,' she said.

'My poor darling! What shall I do? Let me see.
Where do you feel it most.'

'All over. Do you not feel how I shiver? Oh, Ludovic,
could we get out at the next station?'

'Impossible, Linda. What should we do there?'

'And what shall we do at Augsburg? Oh dear, I wish
I had not come. I am so cold. It is killing me.' Then she
burst out into floods of sobbing, so that the old man
opposite to her was aroused. The old man had brandy
in his basket and made her drink a little. Then after a
while she was quieted, and was taken by station after
station without demanding of Ludovic that he should
bring this weary journey to an end.

Gradually the day dawned, and the two could look at

each other in the grey light of the morning. But Linda
thought of her own appearance rather than that of her
lover. She had been taught that it was required of a
woman that she should be neat, and she felt now that she
was dirty, foul inside and out,—a thing to be scorned.
As their companions also bestirred themselves in the
daylight, she was afraid to meet their eyes, and strove to
conceal her face. The sacks in the warehouse had, in
lieu of a better bed, been acceptable; but she was aware
now, as she could see the skirts of her own dress and
her shoes, and as she glanced her eyes gradually round
upon her shoulders, that the stains of the place were upon
her, and she knew herself to be unclean. That sense of
killing cold had passed off from her, having grown to a
numbness which did not amount to present pain, though
it would hardly leave her without some return of the
agony; but the misery of her disreputable appearance
was almost as bad to her as the cold had been. It was
not only that she was untidy and dishevelled, but it was
that her condition should have been such without the
company of any elder female friend whose presence
would have said, 'This young woman is respectable, even
though her dress be soiled with dust and meal.' As it
was, the friend by her side was one who by his very
appearance would condemn her. No one would suppose
her to be his wife. And then the worst of it was that he
also would judge her as others judged her. He also
would say to himself that no one would suppose such a
woman to be his wife. And if once he should learn so to
think of her, how could she expect that he would ever
persuade himself to become her husband? How she
wished that she had remained beneath her aunt's roof!
It now occurred to her, as though for the first time, that
no one could have forced her to go to church on that
thirtieth of January and become Peter Steinmarc's wife.
Why had she not remained at home and simply told her
aunt that the thing was impossible?

At last they were within an hour of Augsburg, and even
yet she knew nothing as to his future plans. It was very
odd that he should not have told her what they were to

do at Augsburg. He said that she should be his queen, that she should be as happy as the day was long, that everything would be right as soon as they reached Augsburg; but now they were all but at Augsburg, and she did not as yet know what first step they were to take when they reached the town. She had much wished that he would speak without being questioned, but at last she thought that she was bound to question him. 'Ludovic, where are we going to at Augsburg?'

'To the Black Bear first. That will be best at first.'

'Is it an inn?'

'Yes, dear; not a great big house like the Rothe Ross at Nuremberg, but very quiet and retired, in a back street.'

'Do they expect us?'

'Well, no; not exactly. But that won't matter.'

'And how long shall we stay there?'

'Ah! that must depend on tidings from Berlin and Munich. It may be that we shall be compelled to get away from Bavaria altogether.' Then he paused for a moment, while she was thinking what other question she could ask. 'By the by,' he said, 'my father is in Augsburg.'

She had heard of his father as a man altogether worthless, one ever in difficulties, who would never work, who had never seemed to wish to be respectable. When the great sins of Ludovic's father had been magnified to her by Madame Staubach and by Peter, with certain wise hints that swans never came out of the eggs of geese, Linda would declare with some pride of spirit that the son was not like the father; that the son had never been known to be idle. She had not attempted to defend the father, of whom it seemed to be acknowledged by the common consent of all Nuremberg that he was utterly worthless, and a disgrace to the city which had produced him. But Linda now felt very thankful for the assurance of even his presence. Had it been Ludovic's mother, how much better would it have been! But that she should be received even by his father,—by such a father,—was much to her in her desolate condition.

'Will he be at the station?' Linda asked.

'Oh, no.'

'Does he expect us?'

'Well, no. You see, Linda, I only got out of prison yesterday morning.'

'Does your father live in Augsburg?'

'He hardly lives anywhere. He goes and comes at present as he is wanted by the cause. It is quite on the cards that we should find that the police have nabbed him. · But I hope not. I think not. When I have seen you made comfortable, and when we have had something to eat and drink, I shall know where to seek him. While I am doing so, you had better lie down.'

She was afraid to ask him whether his father knew, or would suspect, aught as to his bringing a companion, or whether the old man would welcome such a companion for his son. Indeed, she hardly knew how to frame any question that had application to herself. She merely assented to his proposition that she should go to bed at the Black Bear, and then waited for the end of their journey. Early in the morning their fellow-passengers had left them, and they were now alone. But Ludovic distressed her no more by the vehemence of his caresses. He also was tired and fagged and cold and jaded. It is not improbable that he had been meditating whether he, in his present walk of life, had done well to encumber himself with the burden of a young woman.

At last they were at the platform at Augsburg. 'Don't move quite yet,' he said. 'One has to be a little careful.' When she attempted to raise herself she found herself to be so numb that all quickness of motion was out of the question. Ludovic, paying no attention to her, sat back in the carriage, with his cap before his face, looking with eager eyes over the cap on to the platform.

'May we not go now?' said Linda, when she saw that the other passengers had alighted.

'Don't be in a hurry, my girl. By God, there are those ruffians, the gendarmerie. It's all up. By Jove! yes, it's all up. That is hard, after all I did at Nuremberg.'

'Ludovic!'

'Look here, Linda. Get out at once and take these

letters. Make your way to the Black Bear, and wait for me.'

'And you?'

'Never mind me, but do as you're told. In a moment it will be too late. If we are noticed to be together it will be too late.'

'But how am I to get to the Black Bear?'

'Heaven and earth! haven't you a tongue? But here they are, and it's all up.' And so it was. A railway porter opened the door, and behind the railway porter were two policemen. Linda, in her dismay, had not even taken the papers which had been offered to her, and Valcarm, as soon as he was sure that the police were upon him, had stuffed them down the receptacle made in the door for the fall of the window.

But the fate of Valcarm and of his papers is at the present moment not of so much moment to us as is that of Linda Tressel. Valcarm was carried off, with or without the papers, and she, after some hurried words, which were unintelligible to her in her dismay, found herself upon the platform amidst the porters. A message had come from Nuremberg by the wires to Augsburg, requiring the arrest of Ludovic Valcarm, but the wires had said nothing of any companion that might be with him. Therefore Linda was left standing amidst the porters on the platform. She asked one of the men about the Black Bear. He shook his head, and told her that it was a house of a very bad sort,—of a very bad sort indeed.

CHAPTER XII

A DOZEN times during the night Linda had remembered that her old friend Fanny Heisse, now the wife of Max Bogen, lived at Augsburg, and as she remembered it, she had asked herself what she would do were she to meet Fanny in the streets. Would Fanny condescend to speak to her, or would Fanny's husband allow his wife to hold any communion with such a castaway? How might she dare to hope that her old friend would do other than shun her, or, at the very least, scorn her, and pass her as a thing unseen? And yet, through all the days of their life, there had been in Linda's world a supposition that Linda was the good young woman, and that Fanny Heisse was, if not a castaway, one who had made the frivolities of the world so dear to her that she could be accounted as little better than a castaway. Linda's conclusion, as she thought of all this, had been, that it would be better that she should keep out of the way of the wife of an honest man who knew her. All fellowship hereafter with the wives and daughters of honest men must be denied to her. She had felt this very strongly when she had first seen herself in the dawn of the morning.

But now there had fallen upon her a trouble of another kind, which almost crushed her,—in which she was not as yet able to see that, by God's mercy, salvation from utter ruin might yet be extended to her. What should she do now,—now, at this moment? The Black Bear, to which her lover had directed her, was so spoken of that she did not dare to ask to be directed thither. When a compassionate railway porter pressed her to say whither she would go, she could only totter to a seat against the wall, and there lay herself down and sob. She had no friends, she said; no home; no protector except him who had just been carried away to prison. The porter asked her whether the man were her husband, and then again she was nearly choked with sobs. Even the manner of the porter was changed to her when he perceived that she was not the wife of him who had been her companion. He handed her over to an old woman who looked after the station, and the old woman at last learned from Linda the fact that the wife of Max Bogen the lawyer had once been her friend. About two hours after that she was seated with Max Bogen himself, in a small close carriage, and was being taken home to the lawyer's house. Max Bogen asked her hardly a question. He only said that Fanny would be so glad to have her;—Fanny, he said, was so soft, so good, and so clever, and so wise, and always knew exactly what ought to be done. Linda heard it all, marvelling in her dumb half-consciousness.

This was the Fanny Heisse of whom her aunt had so often told her that one so given to the vanities of the world could never come to any good!

Max Bogen handed Linda over to his wife, and then disappeared. 'Oh, Linda, what is it? Why are you here? Dear Linda.' And then her old friend kissed her, and within half an hour the whole story had been told.

'Do you mean that she eloped with him from her aunt's house in the middle of the night?' asked Max, as soon as he was alone with his wife. 'Of course she did,' said Fanny; 'and so would I, had I been treated as she has been. It has all been the fault of that wicked old saint, her aunt.' Then they put their heads together as to the steps that must be taken. Fanny proposed that a letter should be at once sent to Madame Staubach, explaining plainly that Linda had run away from her marriage with Steinmarc, and stating that for the present she was safe and comfortable with her old friend. It could hardly be said that Linda assented to this, because she accepted all that was done for her as a child might accept it. But she knelt upon the floor with her head upon her friend's lap, kissing Fanny's hands, and striving to murmur thanks. Oh, if they would leave her there for three days, so that she might recover something of her strength! 'They shall leave you for three weeks, Linda,' said the other. 'Madame Staubach is not the Emperor, that she is to have her own way in everything. And as for Peter——'

'Pray, don't talk of him;—pray, do not,' said Linda, shuddering.

But all this comfort was at an end about seven o'clock on that evening. The second train in the day from Nuremberg was due at Augsburg at six, and Max Bogen, though he said nothing on the subject to Linda, had thought it probable that some messenger from the former town might arrive in quest of Linda by that train. At seven there came another little carriage up to the door, and before her name could be announced, Madame Staubach was standing in Fanny Bogen's parlour. 'Oh, my child!' she said. 'Oh, my child, may God in His mercy forgive my child!' Linda cowered in a corner of the sofa and did not speak.

'She hasn't done anything in the least wrong,' said Fanny; 'nothing on earth. You were going to make her marry a man she hated, and so she came away. If father had done the same to me, I wouldn't have stayed an hour.' Linda still cowered on the sofa, and was still speechless.

Madame Staubach, when she heard this defence of her niece, was hardly pushed to know in what way it was her duty to answer it. It would be very expedient, of course, that some story should be told for Linda which might save her from the ill report of all the world,—that some excuse should be made which might now, instantly, remove from Linda's name the blight which would make her otherwise to be a thing scorned, defamed, useless, and hideous; but the truth was the truth, and even to save her child from infamy Madame Staubach would not listen to a lie without refuting it. The punishment of Linda's infamy had been deserved, and it was right that it should be endured. Hereafter, as facts came to disclose themselves, it would be for Peter Steinmarc to say whether he would take such a woman for his wife; but whether he took her or whether he rejected her, it could not be well that Linda should be screened by a lie from any part of the punishment which she had deserved. Let her go seven times seven through the fire, if by such suffering there might yet be a chance for her poor desolate half-withered soul.

'Done nothing wrong, Fanny Heisse!' said Madame Staubach, who, in spite of her great fatigue, was still standing in the middle of the room. 'Do you say so, who have become the wife of an honest God-fearing man?'

But Fanny was determined that she would not be put down in her own house by Madame Staubach. 'It doesn't matter whose wife I am,' she said, 'and I am sure Max will say the same as I do. She hasn't done anything wrong. She made up her mind to come away because she wouldn't marry Peter Steinmarc. She came here in company with her own young man, as I used

to come with Max. And as soon as she got here she
sent word up to us, and here she is. If there's anything very wicked in that, I'm not religious enough to
understand it. But I tell you what I can understand,
Madame Staubach,—there is nothing on earth so horribly
wicked as trying to make a girl marry a man whom she
loathes, and hates, and detests, and abominates. There,
Madame Staubach; that's what I've got to say; and now
I hope you'll stop and have supper with Max and Linda
and me.'

Linda felt herself to be blushing in the darkness of her
corner as she heard this excuse for her conduct. No;
she had not made the journey to Augsburg with Ludovic
in such fashion as Fanny had, perhaps more than once,
travelled the same route with her present husband.
Fanny had not come by night, without her father's
knowledge, had not escaped out of a window; nor had
Fanny come with any such purpose as had been hers.
There was no salve to her conscience in all this, though
she felt very grateful to her friend, who was fighting her
battle for her.

'It is not right that I should argue the matter with
you,' said Madame Staubach, with some touch of true
dignity. 'Alas, I know that which I know. Perhaps you
will allow me to say a word in privacy to this unfortunate
child.'

But Max Bogen had not paid his wife a false compliment for cleverness. She perceived at once that the
longer this interview between the aunt and her niece
could be delayed,—the longer that it could be delayed,
now that they were in each other's company,—the
lighter would be the storm on Linda's head when it did
come. 'After supper, Madame Staubach; Linda wants
her supper; don't you, my pet?' Linda answered nothing.
She could not even look up, so as to meet the glance of
her aunt's eyes. But Fanny Bogen succeeded in arranging
things after her own fashion. She would not leave the
room, though in sooth her presence at the preparation
of the supper might have been useful. It came to be
understood that Madame Staubach was to sleep at the

lawyer's house, and great changes were made in order
that the aunt and niece might not be put in the same
room. Early in the morning they were to return together
to Nuremberg, and then Linda's short hour of comfort
would be over.

She had hardly as yet spoken a word to her aunt when
Fanny left them in the carriage together. 'There were
three or four others there,' said Fanny to her husband,
'and she won't have much said to her before she gets
home.'

'But when she is at home!' Fanny only shrugged her
shoulders. 'The truth is, you know,' said Max, 'that it
was not at all the proper sort of thing to do!'

'And who does the proper sort of thing?'

'You do, my dear.'

'And wouldn't you have run away with me if father
had wanted me to marry some nasty old fellow who cares
for nothing but his pipe and his beer? If you hadn't,
I'd never have spoken to you again.'

'All the same,' said Max, 'it won't do her any good.'

The journey home to Nuremberg was made almost in
silence, and things had been so managed by Fanny's craft
that when the two women entered the red house hardly
a word between them had been spoken as to the affairs
of the previous day. Tetchen, as she saw them enter,
cast a guilty glance on her young mistress, but said not a
word. Linda herself, with a veil over her face which she
had borrowed from her friend Fanny, hurried up-stairs
towards her own room. 'Go into my chamber, Linda,'
said Madame Staubach, who followed her. Linda did as
she was bid, went in, and stood by the side of her aunt's
bed. 'Kneel down with me, Linda, and let us pray that
the great gift of repentance may be given to us,' said
Madame Staubach. Then Linda knelt down, and hid
her face upon the counterpane.

All her sins were recapitulated to her during that
prayer. The whole heinousness of the thing which she
had done was given in its full details, and the details
were repeated more than once. It was acknowledged
in that prayer that though God's grace might effect

absolute pardon in the world to come, such a deed as that which had been done by this young woman was beyond the pale of pardon in this world. And the Giver of all mercy was specially asked so to make things clear to that poor sinful creature, that she might not be deluded into any idea that the thing which she had done could be justified. She was told in that prayer that she was impure, vile, unclean, and infamous. And yet she probably did not suffer from the prayer half so much as she would have suffered had the same things been said to her face to face across the table. And she recognised the truth of the prayer, and she was thankful that no allusion was made in it to Peter Steinmarc, and she endeavoured to acknowledge that her conduct was that which her aunt represented it to be in her strong language. When the prayer was over Madame Staubach stood before Linda for a while, and put her two hands on the girl's arms, and lightly kissed her brow. 'Linda,' she said, 'with the Lord nothing is impossible; with the Lord it is never too late; with the Lord the punishment need never be unto death!' Linda, though she could utter no articulate word, acknowledged to herself that her aunt had been good to her, and almost forgot the evil things that her aunt had worked for her.

CHAPTER XIII

LINDA TRESSEL, before she had gone to bed on that night which she had passed at Augsburg, had written a short note which was to be delivered, if such delivery should be possible, to Ludovic Valcarm. The condition of her lover had, of course, been an added trouble to those which were more especially her own. During the last three or four hours which she had passed with him in the train her tenderness for him had been numbed by her own sufferings, and she had allowed herself for a while to think that he was not sufficiently alive to the great sacrifice she was making on his behalf. But when he was removed from her, and had been taken, as she well knew, to the prison of the city, something of the softness of her love returned to her, and she tried to persuade herself that she owed to him that duty which a wife would owe. When she spoke to Fanny on the subject, she declared that even if it were possible to her she would not go back to Ludovic. 'I see it differently now,' she said; 'and I see how bad it is.' But, still,—though she declared that she was very firm in that resolve,—she did not like to be carried back to her old home without doing something, making some attempt, which might be at least a token to herself that she had not been heartless in regard to her lover. She wrote therefore with much difficulty the following few words, which Fanny promised that her husband should endeavour to convey to the hands of Ludovic Valcarm:

'DEAR LUDOVIC,—My aunt has come here for me, and takes me back to Nuremberg to-morrow. When you left me at the station I was too ill to go to the place you told me; so they sent to this house, and my dear, dear friend Fanny Heisse got her husband to come for me, and I am in their house now. Then my aunt came, and she will take me home to-morrow. I am so unhappy that you should be in trouble! I hope that my coming with you did not help to bring it about. As for me, I know it is best that I should go back, though I think that it will kill me. I was very wicked to come. I feel that now, and I know that even you will have ceased to respect me. Dear Ludovic, I hope that God will forgive us both. It will be better that we should never meet again, though the thought that it must be so is almost more than I can bear. I have always felt that I was different from other girls, and that there never could be any happiness for me in this world. God bless you, Ludovic. Think of me some-times,—but never, never, try to come for me again.

L. T.'

It had cost her an hour of hard toil to write this little letter, and when it was written she felt that it was cold, un-grateful, unloving,—very unlike the words which he would feel that he had a right to expect from her. Nevertheless,

such as it was, she gave it to her friend Fanny, with many
injunctions that it might, if possible, be placed in the
hands of Ludovic. And thus, as she told herself repeatedly
on her way home, the romance of her life was over. After
all, the journey to Augsburg would have been serviceable
to her,—would be serviceable although her character
should be infamous for ever in the town that knew her,—
if by that journey she would be saved from all further
mention of the name of Peter Steinmarc. No disgrace
would be so bad as the prospect of that marriage. Therefore, as she journeyed homeward, sitting opposite to her
aunt, she endeavoured to console herself by reflecting
that his suit to her would surely be at an end. Would it
ever reach his dull heart that she had consented to destroy
her own character, to undergo ill-repute and the scorn
of all honest people, in order that she might not be forced
into the horror of a marriage with him? Could he be
made to understand that in her flight from Nuremberg
her great motive had been to fly from him?

On the second morning after her return even this
consolation was taken from her, and she learned from
her aunt that she had not given up all hope in the direction of the town-clerk. On the first day after her return
not a word was said to Linda about Peter, nor would she
have had any notice of his presence in the house had she
not heard his shoes creaking up and down the stairs.
Nor was the name of Ludovic Valcarm so much as
mentioned in her presence. Between Tetchen and her
there was not a word passed, unless such as were spoken
in the presence of Madame Staubach. Linda found that
she was hardly allowed to be for a moment out of her
aunt's presence, and at this time she was unable not to
be submissive. It seemed to her that her aunt was so
good to her in not positively upbraiding her from morning to night, that it was impossible for her not to be
altogether obedient in all things! She did not therefore
even struggle to escape the long readings, and the longer
prayers, and the austere severity of her aunt's presence.
Except in prayer,—in prayers delivered out loud by the
aunt in the niece's presence,—no direct mention was

made of the great iniquity of which Linda had been guilty. Linda was called no heartrending name to her face; but she was required to join, and did join over and over again, in petitions to the throne of mercy 'that the poor castaway might be received back again into the pale of those who were accepted.' And at this time she would have been content to continue to live like this, to join in such prayers day after day, to have her own infamy continually brought forward as needing some special mercy, if by such means she might be allowed to live in tranquillity without sight or mention of Peter Steinmarc. But such tranquillity was not to be hers.

On the afternoon of the second day her aunt went out, leaving Linda alone in the house with Tetchen. Linda at once went to her chamber, and endeavoured to make herself busy among those possessions of her own which she had so lately thought that she was leaving for ever. She took out her all, the articles of her wardrobe, all her little treasures, opened the sweet folds of her modest raiment and refolded them, weeping all the while as she thought of the wreck she had made of herself. But no; it was not she who had made the wreck. She had been ruined by the cruelty of that man whose step at this moment she heard beneath her. She clenched her fist, and pressed her little foot against the floor, as she thought of the injury which this man had done her. There was not enough of charity in her religion to induce her even to think that she would ever cease to hate him with all the vigour of her heart. Then Tetchen came to her, and told her that her aunt had returned and desired to see her. Linda instantly went down to the parlour. Up to this moment she was as a child in her aunt's hands.

'Sit down, Linda,' said Madame Staubach, who had taken off her bonnet, and was already herself stiffly seated in her accustomed chair. 'Sit down, my dear, while I speak to you.' Linda sat down at some distance from her aunt, and awaited dumbly the speech that was to be made to her. 'Linda,' continued Madame Staubach, 'I have been this afternoon to the house of your friend Herr Molk.' Linda said nothing out loud, but she declared to herself that Herr Molk was no friend of hers. Friend indeed! Herr Molk had shown himself to be one of her bitterest enemies. 'I thought it best to see him after what—has been done, especially as he had been with you when you were ill, before you went.' Still Linda said nothing. What was there that she could possibly say? Madame Staubach paused, not expecting her niece to speak, but collecting her own thoughts and arranging her words. 'And Peter Steinmarc was there also,' said Madamé Staubach. Upon hearing this Linda's heart sank within her. Had all her sufferings, then, been for nothing? Had she passed that terrible night, that terrible day, with no result that might be useful to her? But even yet might there not be hope? Was it not possible that her aunt was about to communicate to her the fact that Peter Steinmarc declined to be bound by his engagement to her? She sighed deeply and almost sobbed, as she clasped her hands together. Her aunt observed it all, and then went on with her speech. 'You will, I hope, have understood, Linda, that I have not wished to upbraid you.'

'You have been very good, aunt Charlotte.'

'But you must know that that which you have done is, —is,—is a thing altogether destructive of a young woman's name and character.' Madame Staubach's voice, as she said this, was tremulous with the excess of her eagerness. If this were Peter Steinmarc's decision, Linda would bear it all without a complaint. She bowed her head in token that she accepted the disgrace of which her aunt had spoken. 'Of course, Linda,' continued Madame Staubach, 'recovery from so lamentable a position is very difficult,—is almost impossible. I do not mean to say a word of what has been done. We believe, —that is, I believe, and Herr Molk, and Peter also believes it——'

'I don't care what Peter Steinmarc believes,' exclaimed Linda, unable to hold her peace any longer.

'Linda, Linda, would you be a thing to be shuddered at, a woman without a name, a byword for shame for ever?' Madame Staubach had been interrupted in her

statement as to the belief entertained in respect to
Linda's journey by herself and her two colleagues, and
did not recur to that special point in her narrative. When
Linda made no answer to her last appeal, she broadly
stated the conclusion to which she and her friends had
come in consultation together in the panelled chamber of
Herr Molk's house. 'I may as well make the story short,'
she said. 'Herr Molk has explained to Peter that things
are not as bad as they have seemed to be.' Every muscle
and every fibre in Linda's body was convulsed when she
heard this, and she shuddered and shivered so that she
could hardly keep her seat upon her chair. 'And Peter
has declared that he will be satisfied if you will at once
agree that the marriage shall take place on the thirtieth
of the month. If you will do this, and will make him a
promise that you will go nowhere without his sanction
before that day, he will forget what has been done.'
Linda answered not a word, but burst into tears, and fell
at her aunt's feet.

Madame Staubach was a woman who could bring herself to pardon any sin that had been committed,—that
was done, and, as it were, accomplished,—hoping in all
charity that it would be followed by repentance. Therefore she had forgiven, after a fashion, even the last
tremendous trespass of which her niece had been guilty,
and had contented herself with forcing Linda to listen
to her prayers that repentance might be forthcoming.
But she could forgive no fault, no conduct that seemed
to herself to be in the slightest degree wrong, while it was
in the course of action. She had abstained from all hard
words against Linda, from all rebuke, since she had found
that the young man was gone, and that her niece was
willing to return to her home. But she would be prepared
to exercise all the power which Linda's position had
given her, to be as severe as the austerity of her nature
would permit, if this girl should persist in her obstinacy.
She regarded it as Linda's positive duty to submit to
Peter Steinmarc as her husband. They had been betrothed with Linda's own consent. The banns had been
already once called. She herself had asked for God's

protection over them as man and wife. And then how much was there not due to Peter, who had consented, not without much difficult persuasion from Herr Molk, to take this soiled flower to his bosom, in spite of the darkness of the stain. 'There will be no provoking difficulties made about the house?' Peter had said in a corner to the burgomaster. Then the burgomaster had undertaken that in the circumstances as they now existed, there should be no provoking difficulties. Herr Molk understood that Linda must give up something on receiving that position of an honest man's wife, which she was now hardly entitled to expect. Thus the bargain had been made, and Madame Staubach was of opinion that it was her first duty to see that it should not be again endangered by any obstinacy on behalf of Linda. Obstinate, indeed! How could she be obstinate after that which she had done? She had now fallen at her aunt's feet, was weeping, sobbing, praying for mercy. But Madame Staubach could have no mercy on the girl in this position. Such mercy would in itself be a sin. The sin done she could forgive; the sin a-doing must be crushed, and put down, and burnt out, and extinguished, let the agony coming from such process be as severe as might be. There could be no softness for Linda while Linda was obstinate. 'I cannot suppose,' she said, 'that you mean to hesitate after what has taken place.'

'Oh, aunt Charlotte! dear aunt Charlotte!'

'What is the meaning of this?'

'I don't love him. I can't love him. I will do anything else that you please. He may have the house if he wants it. I will promise;—promise never to go away again or to see anybody.' But she might as well have addressed such prayers to a figure of stone. On such a matter as this Madame Staubach could not be other than relentless. Even while Linda was kneeling at her feet convulsed with sobs, she told the poor girl, with all the severity of language which she could use, of the vileness of the iniquity of that night's proceedings. Linda had been false to her friend, false to her vows, false to her God, immodest, unclean, had sinned against all the laws by which women bind themselves together for good conduct, —had in fact become a castaway in very deed. There was nothing that a female could do more vile, more loathsome than that which Linda had done. Madame Staubach believed that the time had come in which it would be wicked to spare, and she did not spare. Linda grovelled at her feet, and could only pray that God might take her to Himself at once. 'He will never take you; never, never, never,' said Madame Staubach; 'Satan will have you for his own, and all my prayers will be of no avail.'

There were two days such as this, and Linda was still alive and still bore it. On the third day, which was the fifth after her return from Augsburg, Herr Molk came to her, and at his own request was alone with her. He did not vituperate her as her aunt had done, nor did he express any special personal horror at her sin; but he insisted very plainly on the position which she had made for herself. 'You see, my dear, the only thing for you is to be married out of hand at once, and then nobody will say anything about it. And what is the difference if he is a little old? girls forget to think about that after a month or two; and then, you see, it will put an end to all your troubles;—to all your troubles.' Such were the arguments of Herr Molk; and it must be acknowledged that such arguments were not lacking in strength, nor were they altogether without truth. The little story of Linda's journey to Augsburg had been told throughout the city, and there were not wanting many who said that Peter Steinmarc must be a very good-natured man indeed, if, after all that had passed, he would still accept Linda Tressel as his wife. 'You should remember all that of course, my dear,' said Herr Molk.

How was it possible that Linda should stand alone against such influence as had been brought to bear against her? She was quite alone, for she would not admit of any intimacy with Tetchen. She would hardly speak to the old woman. She was quite aware that Tetchen had arranged with Ludovic the manner of her elopement; and though she felt no anger with him, still she was angry with the servant whose duplicity had helped to bring about the present misery. Had she not fled with her lover she might then,—so she thought now, —have held her ground against her aunt and against Peter. As things had gone with her since, such obstinacy had become impossible to her. On the morning of the seventh day she bowed her head, and though she did not speak, she gave her aunt to understand that she had yielded. 'We will begin to purchase what may be necessary to-morrow,' said Madame Staubach.

But even now she had not made up her mind that she would in truth marry the man. She had simply found it again impossible to say that she would not do so. There was still a chance of escape. She might die, for instance! Or she might run away again. If she did that, surely the man would persecute her no further. Or at the last moment she might stolidly decline to move; she might refuse to stand on her legs before the altar. She might be as a dead thing even though she were alive,—as a thing dead and speechless. Oh! if she could only be without ears to hear those terrible words which her aunt would say to her! And then there came another scheme into her mind. She would make one great personal appeal to Steinmarc's feelings as a man. If she implored him not to make her his wife, kneeling before him, submitting herself to him, preferring to him with all her earnestness this one great prayer, surely he would not persevere!

Hitherto, since her return from Augsburg, Peter had done very little to press his own suit. She had again had her hand placed in his since she had yielded, and had accepted as a present from him a great glass brooch which to her eyes was the ugliest thing in the guise of a trinket which the world of vanity had ever seen. She had not been a moment in his company without her aunt's presence, and there had not been the slightest allusion made by him to her elopement. Peter had considered that such allusion had better come after marriage when his power would, as he thought, be consolidated. He was surprised when he was told, early in the morning after that second hand-pledging, by Linda herself that she wanted to see him. Linda came to his door and made her request in person. Of course he was delighted to welcome his future bride to his own apartment, and begged her with as soft a smile as he could assume to seat herself in his own arm-chair. She took a humbler seat, however, and motioned to him to take that to which he was accustomed. He looked at her as he did so, and perceived that the very nature of her face was changed. She had lost the plumpness of her cheeks, she had lost the fresh colour of her youth, she had lost much of her prettiness. But her eyes were brighter than ever they had been, and there was something in their expression which almost made Peter uneasy. Though she had lost so much of her prettiness, he was not on that account moved to doubt the value of his matrimonial prize; but there did come across his mind an idea that those eyes might perhaps bring with them some discomfort into his household. 'I am very glad to see you, Linda,' he said. 'It is very good of you to come to me here. Is there anything I can do for you?'

'There is one thing, Peter Steinmarc, that you can do for me.'

'What is that, my dear?'

'Let me alone.' As she spoke she clenched her small fist and brought it down with some energy on the table that was close to her. She looked into his face as she did so, and his eyes quailed before her glance. Then she repeated her demand. 'Let me alone.'

'I do not know what you mean, Linda. Of course you are going to be my wife now.'

'I do not wish to be your wife. You know that; and if you are a man you will not force me.' She had intended to be gentle with him, to entreat him, to win him by humility and softness, and to take his hand, and even kiss it if he would be good to her. But there was so much of tragedy in her heart, and such an earnestness of purpose in her mind, that she could not be gentle. As she spoke it seemed to him that she was threatening him.

'It is all settled, Linda. It cannot be changed now.'

'It can be changed. It must be changed. Tell her that

I am not good enough. You need not fear her. And if
you will say so, I will never be angry with you for the
word. I will bless you for it.'

'But, Linda, you did nothing so very much amiss;—
did you?' Then there came across her mind an idea that
she would lie to him, and degrade herself with a double
disgrace. But she hesitated, and was not actress enough
to carry on the part. He winked at her as he continued
to speak. 'I know,' he said. 'It was just a foolish business,
but no worse than that.'

Oh heavens, how she hated him! She could have
stabbed him to the heart that moment, had the weapon
been there, and had she possessed the physical energy
necessary for such an enterprise. He was a thing to her
so foul that all her feminine nature recoiled from the
closeness of his presence, and her flesh crept as she felt
that the same atmosphere encompassed them. And this
man was to be her husband! She must speak to him,
speak out, speak very plainly. Could it be possible
that a man should wish to take a woman to his bosom
who had told him to his face that he was loathed? 'Peter,'
she said, 'I am sure that you don't think that I love you.'

'I don't see why you shouldn't, Linda.'

'I do not;—not the least; I can promise you that. And
I never shall;—never. Think what it would be to have
a wife who doesn't love you a bit. Would not that be
bad?'

'Oh, but you will.'

'Never! Don't you know that I love somebody else
very dearly?' On hearing this there came something of
darkness upon Peter's brow,—something which indicated
that he had been touched. Linda understood it all.
'But I will never speak to him again, never see him, if
you will let me alone.'

'See him, Linda! He is in prison, and will be sent to
the quarries to work. He will never be a free man again.
Ha! ha! I need not fear him, my dear.'

'But you shall fear me. Yes; I will lead you such a life!
Peter Steinmarc, I will make you rue the day you first
saw me. You shall wish that you were at the quarries

yourself. I will disgrace you, and make your name infamous. I will waste everything that you have. There is nothing so bad I will not do to punish you. Yes; you may look at me, but I will. Do you think that you are to trample me under foot, and that I will not have my revenge? You said it was a foolish business that I did. I will make it worse than foolish.' He stood with his hands in the pockets of his broad flaps, looking at her, not knowing how to answer her. He was no coward,—not such a coward as to be intimidated at the moment by the girl's violence. And being now thoroughly angry, her words had not worked upon him as she had intended that they should work. His desire was to conquer her and get the best of her; but his thoughts worked slowly, and he did not know how to answer her. 'Well, what do you say to me? If you will let me escape, I will always be your friend.'

'I will not let you escape,' he said.

'And you expect that I shall be your wife?'

'I do expect it.'

'I shall die first; yes;—die first. To be your wife! Oh, there is not a beggar in the streets of Nuremberg whom I would not sooner take for my husband.' She paused, but again he was at a loss for words. 'Come, Peter, think of it. Do not drive a poor weak girl to desperation. I have been very unhappy,—very; you do not know how unhappy I have been. Do not make it worse for me.' Then the chord which had been strung so tightly was broken asunder. Her strength failed her, and she burst into tears.

'I will make you pay dearly for all this one of these days, fraulein,' said Peter, as, with his hands still in his pockets, he left the room. She watched him as he creaked down-stairs, and went into her aunt's apartments. For a moment she felt disposed to go and confront him there before her aunt. Together, the two of them, could not force her to marry him. But her courage failed her. Though she could face Peter Steinmarc without flinching, she feared the words which her aunt could say to her. She had not scrupled to threaten Steinmarc

with her own disgrace, but she could not endure to be
told by her aunt that she was degraded.

CHAPTER XIV

PETER STEINMARC, when he went into Madame Staubach's parlour, found that lady on her knees in prayer.
He had entered the room without notice, having been
urged to this unwonted impetuosity by the severity of the
provocation which he had received. Madame Staubach
raised her head; but when she saw him she did not rise.
He stood there for some seconds looking at her, expecting
her to get up and greet him; but when he found that such
was not her purpose, he turned angrily on his heel, and
went out of the house, up to his office in the town-hall.
His services were not of much service to the city on that
day,—neither on that day nor on the two following days.
He was using all his mental faculties in endeavouring to
decide what it might be best for him to do in the present
emergency. The red house was a chattel of great value
in Nuremberg,—a thing very desirable,—the possession
of which Peter himself did desire with all his heart. But
then, even in regard to the house, it was not to be arranged
that Peter was to become the sole and immediate possessor of it on his marriage. Madame Staubach was to live
there, and during her life the prize would be but a half-
and-half possession. Madame Staubach was younger
than himself; and though he had once thought of marrying her, he was not sure that he was now desirous of
living in the same house with her for the remainder of his
life. He had wished to marry Linda Tressel, because she
was young, and was acknowledged to be a pretty girl;
and he still wished to marry her, if not now for these
reasons, still for others which were quite as potent. He
wanted to be her master, to get the better of her, to
punish her for her disdain of him, and to bring her to his
feet. But he was not a man so carried away by anger or
by a spirit of revenge as to be altogether indifferent to his
own future happiness. There had already been some

among his fellow-citizens, or perhaps citizenesses, kind enough to compliment him on his good-nature. He had been asked whether Linda Tressel had told him all about her little trip to Augsburg, and whether he intended to ask his cousin Ludovic Valcarm to come to his wedding. And now Linda herself had said things to him which made him doubt whether she was fit to be the wife of a man so respectable and so respected as himself. And were she to do those things which she threatened, where would he be then? All the town would laugh at him, and he would be reduced to live for the remainder of his days in the sole company of Madame Staubach as the result of his enterprise. He was sufficiently desirous of being revenged on Linda, but he was a cautious man, and began to think that he might buy even that pleasure too dear. He had been egged on to the marriage by Herr Molk and one or two others of the city pundits,—by the very men whose opposition he had feared when the idea of marrying Linda was first suggested to him. They had told him that Linda was all right, that the elopement had been in point of fact nothing. 'Young girls will be young before they are settled,' Herr Molk had said. Then the extreme desirability of the red house had been mentioned, and so Peter had been persuaded. But now, as the day drew near, and as Linda's words sounded in his ears, he hardly knew what to think of it. On the evening of the third day of his contemplation, he went again to his friend Herr Molk.

'Nonsense, Peter,' said the magistrate; 'you must go on now, and there is no reason why you should not. Is a man of your standing to be turned aside by a few idle words from a young girl?'

'But she told me—— You can't understand what she told me. She's been away with this young fellow once, and she said as much as that she'd go again.'

'Pshaw! you haven't had to do with women as I have, or you would understand them better. Of course a young girl likes to have her little romance. But when a girl has been well brought up,—and there is no better bringing up than what Linda Tressel has had,—marriage

steadies them directly. Think of the position you'll have
in the city when the house belongs to yourself.'

Peter, when he left the magistrate, was still tossed
about by an infinity of doubts. If he should once take
the girl as his wife, he could never unmarry himself
again. He could not do so at least without trouble, disgrace, and ruinous expense. As for revenge, he thought
that he might still have a certain amount of that pleasure
in repudiating his promised spouse for her bad conduct,
and in declaring to her aunt that he could not bring
himself to make a wife of a woman who had first disgraced herself, and then absolutely taken glory in her
disgrace. As he went along from Herr Molk's house
towards the island, taking a somewhat long path by the
Rothe Ross where he refreshed himself, and down the
Carls Strasse, and by the Church of St. Lawrence, round
which he walked twice, looking up to the tower for
inspiration,—he told himself that circumstances had been
most cruel to him. He complained bitterly of his misfortune. If he refused to marry Linda he must leave the
red house altogether, and would, of course, be ridiculed
for his attempt at matrimony; and if he did marry her
—— Then, as far as he could see, there would be the very
mischief. He pitied himself with an exceedingly strong
compassion, because of the unmerited hardness of his
position. It was very dark when he got to the narrow
passage leading to the house along the river, and when
there, in the narrowest and darkest part of the passage,
whom should he meet coming from Madame Staubach's
house,—coming from Linda's house, for the passage led
from the red house only,—but Ludovic Valcarm his
cousin?

'What, uncle Peter?' said Ludovic, assuming a name
which he had sometimes used in old days when he had
wished to be impertinent to his relative. Peter Steinmarc
was too much taken aback to have any speech ready on
the occasion. 'You don't say a word to congratulate me
on having escaped from the hands of the Philistines.'

'What are you doing here?' said Peter.

'I've been to see my young woman,' said Ludovic,

who, as Peter imagined, was somewhat elated by strong drink.

'She is not your young woman,' said Peter.

'She is not yours at any rate,' said the other.

'She is mine if I like to take her,' said Peter.

'We shall see about that. But here I am again, at any rate. The mischief take them for interfering old fools! When they had got me they had nothing to say against me.'

'Pass on, and let me go by,' said Peter.

'One word first, uncle Peter. Among you, you are treating that girl as cruelly as ever a girl was treated. You had better be warned by me, and leave off. If she were forced into a marriage with you, you would only disgrace yourself. I don't suppose you want to see her dead at your feet. Go on now, and think of what I have said to you.' So Ludovic had been with her again! No; he, Peter Steinmarc, would not wed with one who was so abandoned. He would reject her;—would reject her that very night. But he would do so in a manner that should leave her very little cause for joy or triumph.

We must now go back for a while to Linda and her aunt. No detailed account of that meeting between Linda and Steinmarc, in Steinmarc's room, ever reached Madame Staubach's ears. That there had been an interview, and that Linda had asked Steinmarc to absolve her from her troth, the aunt did learn from the niece; and most angry she was when she learned it. She again pointed out to the sinner the terrible sin of which she was guilty in not submitting herself entirely, in not eradicating and casting out from her bosom all her human feelings, in not crushing herself, as it were, upon a wheel, in token of her repentance for what she had done. Sackcloth and ashes, in their material shape, were odious to the imagination of Madame Staubach, because they had a savour of Papacy, and implied that the poor sinner who bore them could do something towards his own salvation by his own works; but that moral sackcloth, and those ashes of the heart and mind, which she was ever prescribing to Linda, seemed to her to have none of this taint. And yet, in what is the difference? The school of religion to which Madame Staubach belonged was very like that early school of the Church of Rome in which material ashes were first used for the personal annoyance of the sinner. But the Church of Rome in Madame Staubach's day had, by the force of the human nature of its adherents, made its way back to the natural sympathies of mankind; whereas in Madame Staubach's school the austerity of self-punishment was still believed to be all in all. During the days of Steinmarc's meditation, Linda was prayed for and was preached to with an unflagging diligence which, at the end of that time, had almost brought the girl to madness. For Linda the worst circumstance of all was this, that she had never as yet brought herself to disbelieve her aunt's religious menaces. She had been so educated that what fixed belief she had on the subject at all was in accordance with her aunt's creed rather than against it. When she was alone, she would tell herself that it was her lot to undergo that eternal condemnation with which her aunt threatened her; though in telling herself so she would declare to herself also that whatever that punishment could be, her Creator, let Him be ever so relentless, could inflict nothing on her worse than that state of agony with which His creatures had tormented her in this world.

She was in this state when Tetchen crept up to her room, on that evening on which Peter had been with Herr Molk. 'Fraulein,' said Tetchen, 'you are very unkind to me.'

'Never mind,' said Linda, not looking up into the woman's face.

'I have done everything in my power for you, as though you had been my own.'

'I am not your own. I don't want you to do anything for me.'

'I love you dearly, and I love him,—Ludovic. Have I not done everything in my power to save you from the man you hate?'

'You made me go off with him in the night, like a— like a——! Oh, Tetchen, was that treating me as though

I had been your own? Would you have done that for your own child?'

'Why not,—if you are to be his wife?'

'Tetchen, you have made me hate you, and you have made me hate myself. If I had not done that, I should not be such a coward. Go away. I do not want to speak to you.'

Then the old woman came close up to Linda, and stood for a moment leaning over her. Linda took no notice of her, but continued by a certain tremulous shaking of her knee to show how strongly she was moved. 'My darling,' said Tetchen, 'why should you send away from you those who love you?'

'Nobody loves me,' said Linda.

'I love you,—and Ludovic loves you.'

'That is of no use,—of none at all. I do not wish to hear his name again. It was not his fault, but he has disgraced me. It was my own fault,—and yours.'

'Linda, he is in the house now.'

'Who,—Ludovic?'

'Yes; Ludovic Valcarm.'

'In the house? How did he escape?'

'They could do nothing to him. They let him go. They were obliged to let him go.'

Then Linda got up from her seat, and stood for a minute with her eyes fixed upon the old woman's face, thinking what step she had better take. In the confusion of her mind, and in the state to which she had been reduced, there was no idea left with her that it might yet be possible that she would become the wife of Ludovic Valcarm, and live as such the life of a respectable woman. She had taught herself to acknowledge that her elopement with him had made that quite impossible;—that by what they had done they had both put themselves beyond the pale of such gentle mercy. Such evil had come to her from her secret interviews with this man who had become her lover almost without her own acquiescence, that she dreaded him even though she loved him. The remembrance of the night she had passed with him, partly in the warehouse and partly in the railway train, had nothing in it of the sweetness of love, to make her thoughts of it acceptable to her. This girl was so pure at heart, was by her own feelings so prone to virtue, that she looked back upon what she had done with abhorrence. Whether she had sinned or not, she hated what she had done as though it had been sinful; and now, when she was told that Ludovic Valcarm was again in the house, she recoiled from the idea of meeting him. On the former occasions of his coming to her, a choice had hardly been allowed to her whether she would see him or not. He had been with her before she had had time to fly from him. Now she had a moment for thought,—a moment in which she could ask herself whether it would be good for her to place herself again in his hands. She said that it would not be good, and she walked steadily down to her aunt's parlour. 'Aunt Charlotte,' she said, 'Ludovic Valcarm is in the house.'

'In this house,—again!' exclaimed Madame Staubach. Linda, having made her statement, said not a word further. Though she had felt herself compelled to turn informant against her lover, and by implication against Tetchen, her lover's accomplice, nevertheless she despised herself for what she was doing. She did not expect to soften her aunt by her conduct, or in any way to mitigate the rigour of her own sufferings. Her clandestine meetings with Ludovic had brought with them so much of pain and shame, that she had resolved almost by instinct to avoid another. But having taken this step to avoid it, she had nothing further to say or to do. 'Where is the young man?' demanded Madame Staubach.

'Tetchen says that he is here, in the house,' said Linda. Then Madame Staubach left the parlour, and crossed into the kitchen. There, standing close to the stove and warming himself, she found this terrible youth who had worked her so much trouble. It seemed to Madame Staubach that for months past she had been hearing of his having been constantly in and about the house, entering where he would and when he would, and in all those months she had never seen him. When last she had beheld him he had been to her simply a foolish idle youth with whom his elder cousin had been forced to quarrel. Since that, he had become to her a source of infinite terror. He had been described to her as one guilty of crimes which, much as she hated them, produced, even in her breast, a kind of respect for the criminal. He was a rebel of whom the magistrates were afraid. When in prison he had had means of escaping. When arrested at Nuremberg he would be the next day at Augsburg; when arrested at Augsburg he would be the next day at Nuremberg. He could get in and out of the roofs of houses, and could carry away with him a young maiden. These are deeds which always excite a certain degree of admiration in the female heart, and Madame Staubach, though she was a Baptist, was still a female. When, therefore, she found herself in the presence of Ludovic, she could not treat him with the indignant scorn with which she would have received him had he intruded upon her premises before her fears of him had been excited. 'Why are you here, Ludovic Valcarm?' she said advancing hardly a step beyond the doorway. Ludovic looked up at her with his hand resting on the table. He was not drunk, but he had been drinking; his clothes were soiled; he was unwashed and dirty, and the appearance of the man was that of a vagabond. 'Speak to me, and tell me why you are here,' said Madame Staubach.

'I have come to look for my wife,' said Ludovic.

'You have no wife;—at any rate you have none here.'

'Linda Tressel is my true and lawful wife, and I have come to take her away with me. She went with me once, and now she will go again. Where is she? You're not going to keep her locked up. It's against the law to make a young woman a prisoner.'

'My niece does not wish to see you;—does not intend to see you. Go away.'

But he refused to go, and threatened her, alleging that Linda Tressel was of an age which allowed her to dispose as she pleased of her person and her property. Of course this was of no avail with Madame Staubach, who was determined that, whatever might happen, the young man

should not force himself into Linda's presence. When
Ludovic attempted to leave the kitchen, Madame Staubach stood in the doorway and called for Tetchen. The
servant, who had perched herself on the landing, since
Linda had entered the parlour, was down in a moment,
and with various winks and little signs endeavoured to
induce Valcarm to leave the house. 'You had better go,
or I shall call at once for my neighbour Jacob Heisse,'
said Madame Staubach. Then she did call, as lustily as
she was able, though in vain. Upon this Ludovic, not
knowing how to proceed, unable or unwilling to force
his way further into the house in opposition to Madame
Staubach, took his departure, and as he went met Peter
Steinmarc in the passage at the back of Heisse's house.
Madame Staubach was still in the kitchen asking questions of Tetchen which Tetchen did not answer with
perfect truth, when Peter appeared among them.
'Madame Staubach,' he said, 'that vagabond Ludovic
Valcarm has just been here, in this house.'

'He went away but a minute since,' said Madame
Staubach.

'Just so. That is exactly what I mean. This is a thing
not to be borne,—not to be endured, and shows that
your niece Linda is altogether beyond the reach of any
good impressions.'

'Peter Steinmarc!'

'Yes, that is all very well; of course I expect that you
will take her part; although, with your high ideas of
religion and all that sort of thing, it is almost unaccount-
able that you should do so. As far as I am concerned
there must be an end of it. I am not going to make myself
ridiculous to all Nuremberg by marrying a young woman
who has no sense whatever of self-respect. I have over-
looked a great deal too much already,—a great deal too
much.'

'But Linda has not seen the young man. It was she
herself who told me that he was here.'

'Ah, very well. I don't know anything about that. I
saw him coming away from here, and it may be as well
to tell you that I have made up my mind. Linda Tressel

is not the sort of young woman that I took her to be, and I shall have nothing more to say to her.'

'You are an old goose,' said Tetchen.

'Hold your tongue,' said Madame Staubach angrily to her servant. Though she was very indignant with Peter Steinmarc, still it would go much against the grain with her that the match should be broken off. She had resolved so firmly that this marriage was proper for all purposes, that she had almost come to look at it as though it were a thing ordained of God. Then, too, she remembered, even in this moment, that Peter Steinmarc had received great provocation. Her immediate object was to persuade him that nothing had been done to give him further provocation. No fault had been committed by Linda which had not already been made known to him and been condoned by him. But how was she to explain all this to him in privacy, while Tetchen was in the kitchen, and Linda was in the parlour opposite? 'Peter, on my word as an honest truthful woman, Linda has been guilty of no further fault.'

'She has been guilty of more than enough,' said Peter.

'That may be said of all us guilty, frail, sinful human beings,' rejoined Madame Staubach.

'I doubt whether there are any of us so bad as she is,' said Peter.

'I wonder, madame, you can condescend to argue with him,' said Tetchen; 'as if all the world did not know that the fraulein is ten times too good for the like of him!'

'Hold your tongue,' said Madame Staubach.

'And where is Miss Linda at the present moment?' demanded Peter. Madame Staubach hesitated for an instant before she answered, and then replied that Linda was in the parlour. It might seem, she thought, that there was some cause for secrecy if she made any concealment at the present moment. Then Peter made his way out of the kitchen and across the passage, and without any invitation entered the parlour. Madame Staubach followed him, and Tetchen followed also. It was unfortunate for Madame Staubach's plans that the meeting between Peter and Linda should take place in this way, but she

could not help it. But she was already making up her
mind to this,—that if Peter Steinmarc ill-treated her
niece, she would bring all Nuremberg about his ears.

'Linda Tressel,' he said;—and as he spoke, the impetuosity of indignation to which he had worked himself
had not as yet subsided, and therefore he was full of
courage;—'Linda Tressel, I find that that vagabond
Ludovic Valcarm has again been here.'

'He is no vagabond,' said Linda, turning upon him
with full as much indignation as his own.

'All the city knows him, and all the city knows you
too. You are no better than you should be, and I wash
my hands of you.'

'Let it be so,' said Linda; 'and for such a blessing I
will pardon you the unmanly cruelty of your words.'

'But I will not pardon him,' said Madame Staubach.
'It is false; and if he dares to repeat such words, he shall
rue them as long as he lives. Linda, this is to go for
nothing,—for nothing. Perhaps it is not unnatural that
he should have some suspicion.' Poor Madame Staubach,
agitated by divided feelings, hardly knew on which side
to use her eloquence.

'I should think not indeed,' said Peter, in triumph.
'Unnatural! Ha! ha!'

'I will put his eyes out of him if he laughs like that,'
said Tetchen, looking as though she were ready to put
her threat into execution upon the instant.

'Peter Steinmarc, you are mistaken in this,' said
Madame Staubach. 'You had better let me see you in
private.'

'Mistaken, am I? Oh! am I mistaken in thinking that
she was alone during the whole night with Ludovic? A
man does not like such mistakes as that. I tell you that I
have done with her,—done with her,—done with her!
She is a bad piece. She does not ring sound. Madame
Staubach, I respect you, and am sorry for you; but you
know the truth as well as I do.'

'Man,' she said to him, 'you are ungrateful, cruel, and
unjust.'

'Aunt Charlotte,' said Linda, 'he has done me the only

favour that I could accept at his hands. It is true that I have done that which, had he been a man, would have prevented him from seeking to make me his wife. All that is true. I own it.'

'There; you hear her, Madame Staubach.'

'And you shall hear me by-and-by,' said Madame Staubach.

'But it is no thought of that that has made him give me up,' continued Linda. 'He knows that he never could have got my hand. I told him that I would die first, and he has believed me. It is very well that he should give me up; but no one else, no other man alive, would have been base enough to have spoken to any woman as he has spoken to me.'

'It is all very well for you to say so,' said Peter.

'Aunt Charlotte, I hope I may never be asked to hear another word from his lips, or to speak another word to his ears.' Then Linda escaped from the room, thinking as she went that God in His mercy had saved her at last.

CHAPTER XV

ALL January had passed by. That thirtieth of January had come and gone which was to have made Linda Tressel a bride, and Linda was still Linda Tressel. But her troubles were not therefore over, and Peter Steinmarc was once again her suitor. It may be remembered how he had reviled her in her aunt's presence, how he had reminded her of her indiscretion, and how he had then rejected her; but, nevertheless, in the first week of February he was again her suitor.

Madame Staubach had passed a very troubled and uneasy month. Though she was minded to take her niece's part when Linda was so ungenerously attacked by the man whom she had warmed in the bosom of her family, still she was most unwilling that Linda should triumph. Her feminine instincts prompted her to take Linda's part on the spur of the moment, as similar instincts had prompted Tetchen to do the same thing;

but hardly the less on that account did she feel that it was still her duty to persevere with that process of crushing by which all human vanity was to be pressed out of Linda's heart. Peter Steinmarc had misbehaved himself grossly, had appeared at that last interview in a guise which could not have made him fascinating to any young woman; but on that account the merit of submitting to him would be so much the greater. There could hardly be any moral sackcloth and ashes too coarse and too bitter for the correction of a sinful mind in this world, but for the special correction of a mind sinful as Linda's had been, marriage with such a man as Peter Steinmarc would be sackcloth and ashes of the most salutary kind. The objection which Linda would feel for the man would be the exact antidote to the poison with which she had been infected by the influence of the Evil One. Madame Staubach acknowledged, when she was asked the question, that a woman should love her husband; but she would always go on to describe this required love as a feeling which should spring from a dutiful submission. She was of opinion that a virtuous child would love his parent, that a virtuous servant would love her mistress, that a virtuous woman would love her husband, even in spite of austere severity on the part of him or her who might be in authority. When, therefore, Linda would refer to what had taken place in the parlour, and would ask whether it were possible that she should love a man who had ill-used her so grossly, Madame Staubach would reply as though love and forgiveness were one and the same thing. It was Linda's duty to pardon the ill-usage and to kiss the rod that had smitten her. 'I hate him so deeply that my blood curdles at the sight of him,' Linda had replied. Then Madame Staubach had prayed that her niece's heart might be softened, and had called upon Linda to join her in these prayers. Poor Linda had felt herself compelled to go down upon her knees and submit herself to such prayer as well as she was able. Could she have enfranchised her mind altogether from the trammels of belief in her aunt's peculiar religion, she might have escaped from the waters which seemed from day to day to be closing over her head; but this was not within her power. She asked herself no questions as to the truth of these convictions. The doctrine had been taught to her from her youth upwards, and she had not realised the fact that she possessed any power of rejecting it. She would tell herself, and that frequently, that to her religion held out no comfort, that she was not of the elect, that manifestly she was a castaway, and that therefore there could be no reason why she should endure unnecessary torments in this life. With such impressions on her mind she had suffered herself to be taken from her aunt's house, and carried off by her lover to Augsburg. With such impressions strong upon her, she would not hesitate to declare her hatred for the man, whom, in truth, she hated with all her heart, but whom, nevertheless, she thought it was wicked to hate. She daily told herself that she was one given up by herself to Satan. But yet, when summoned to her aunt's prayers, when asked to kneel and implore her Lord and Saviour to soften her own heart,—so to soften it that she might become a submissive wife to Peter Steinmarc,—she would comply, because she still believed that such were the sacrifices which a true religion demanded. But there was no comfort to her in her religion. Alas! alas! let her turn herself which way she might, there was no comfort to be found on any side.

At the end of the first week in February no renewed promise of assent had been extracted from Linda; but Peter, who was made of stuff less stern, had been gradually brought round to see that he had been wrong. Madame Staubach had, in the first instance, obtained the co-operation of Herr Molk and others of the leading city magistrates. The question of Linda's marriage had become quite a city matter. She had been indiscreet; that was acknowledged. As to the amount of her indiscretion, different people had different opinions. In the opinion of Herr Molk, that was a thing that did not signify. Linda Tressel was the daughter of a city officer who had been much respected. Her father's successor in that office was just the man who ought to be her husband.

Of course he was a little old and rusty; but then Linda
had been indiscreet. Linda had not only been indiscreet,
but her indiscretion had been, so to say, very public.
She had run away from the city in the middle of the
night with a young man,—with a young man known to
be a scamp and a rebel. It must be acknowledged that
indiscretion could hardly go beyond this. But then was
there not the red house to make things even, and was it
not acknowledged on all sides that Peter Steinmarc was
very rusty?—The magistrates had made up their minds
that the bargain was a just one, and as it had been made,
they thought that it should be carried out. When Peter
complained of further indiscretion on the part of Linda,
and pointed out that he was manifestly absolved from
his contract by her continued misconduct, Herr Molk
went to work with most demure diligence, collected all
the evidence, examined all the parties, and explained to
Peter that Linda had not misbehaved herself since the
contract had last been ratified. 'Peter, my friend,' said
the burgomaster, 'you have no right to go back to anything,—to anything that happened before the twenty-
third.' The twenty-third was the day on which Peter
had expressed his pardon for the great indiscretion of the
elopement. 'Since that time there has been no breach of
trust on her part. I have examined all the parties, Peter.'
It was in vain that Steinmarc tried to show that he was
entitled to be absolved because Linda had said that she
hated him. Herr Molk did not lose above an hour or
two in explaining to him that little amenities of that kind
were to be held as compensated in full by the possession
of the red house. And then, had it not been acknowledged that he was very rusty,—a man naturally to be
hated by a young woman who had shown that she had
a preference for a young lover? 'Oh, bah!' said Herr
Molk, almost angry at this folly; 'do not let me hear
anything more about that, Peter.' Steinmarc had been
convinced, had assented, and was now ready to accept
the hand of his bride.

Nothing more had been heard of Ludovic since the
day on which he had come to the house and had dis-

appeared. Herr Molk, when he was interrogated on the subject, would shake his head, but in truth Herr Molk knew nothing. It was the fact that Valcarm, after being confined in prison at Augsburg for three days, had been discharged by the city magistrates; and it was the case, also, though the fact was not generally known, that the city magistrates of Augsburg had declared the city magistrates of Nuremberg to be——geese. Ludovic Valcarm was not now in prison, but he had left Nuremberg, and no one knew whither he was gone. The brewers, Sach, by whom he had been employed, professed that they knew nothing respecting him; but then, as Herr Molk declared, the two brothers Sach were men who ought themselves to be in prison. They, too, were rebels, according to Herr Molk.

But in truth, as regarded Linda, no trouble need have been taken in inquiring after Ludovic. She made no inquiry respecting him. She would not even listen to Tetchen when Tetchen would suggest this or that mode of ascertaining where he might be. She had allowed herself to be reconciled to Tetchen, because Tetchen had taken her part against Peter Steinmarc; but she would submit to no intrigue at the old woman's instance. 'I do not want to see him ever again, Tetchen.'

'But, fraulein, you loved him.'

'Yes, and I do. But of what use is such love? I could do him no good. If he were there, opposite,—where he used to be,—I would not cross the river to him.'

'I hope, my dear, that it mayn't be so with you always, that's all,' Tetchen had said. But Linda had no vestige of such hope at her heart. The journey to Augsburg had been to her the cause of too much agony, had filled her with too real a sense of maidenly shame, to enable her to look forward with hope to any adventure in which Ludovic should have to take a part. To escape from Peter Steinmarc, whether by death, or illness, or flight, or sullen refusal,—but to escape from him let the cost to herself be what it might,—that was all that she now desired. But she thought that escape was not possible to her. She was coming at last to believe that she would have to stand up in the church and give her hand. If it were so, all Nuremberg should ring with the tragedy of their nuptials.

Since Peter had returned, and expressed to Madame Staubach his willingness to go on with the marriage, he had, after a fashion, been again taken into that lady's favour. He had behaved very badly, but a fault repented was a fault to be forgiven. 'I am sorry that there was a rumpus, Madame Staubach,' he had said, 'but you see that there is so much to put a man's back up when a girl runs away with a man in the middle of the night, you know.'

'Peter,' the widow had replied, interrupting him, 'that need not be discussed again. The wickedness of the human heart is so deep that it cannot be fathomed; but we have the word of the Lord to show to us that no sinner is too vile to be forgiven. What you said in your anger was cruel and unmanly, but it has been pardoned.' Then Peter sat down and lighted his pipe. He did not like the tone of his friend's remarks, but he knew well that there was nothing to be gained by discussing such matters with Madame Staubach. It was better for him to take his old seat quietly, and at once to light his pipe. Linda, on that occasion, and on many others subsequently, came and sat in the room, and there would be almost absolute silence. There might be a question asked about the household, and Linda would answer it; or Peter might remark that such a one among the small city dealers had been fined before the magistrates for some petty breach of the city's laws. But of conversation there was none, and Peter never on these evenings addressed himself specially to Linda. It was quite understood that she was to undergo persuasion, not from Peter, but from her aunt.

About the middle of February her aunt made her last attack on poor Linda. For days before something had been said daily; some word had been spoken in which Madame Staubach alluded to the match as an affair which would certainly be brought about sooner or later. And there were prayers daily for the softening of Linda's heart. And it was understood that every one in the house was supposed to be living under some special cloud of God's anger till Linda's consent should have been given. Madame Staubach had declared during the ecstasy of her devotion, that not only she herself, but even Tetchen also, would become the prey of Satan if Linda did not relent. Linda had almost acknowledged to herself that she was in the act of bringing eternal destruction on all those around her by her obstinacy. Oh, if she could only herself be dead, let the eternal consequences as they regarded herself alone be what they might!

'Linda,' said her aunt, 'is it not time at length that you should give us an answer?'

'An answer, aunt Charlotte?' As if she had not given a sufficiency of answers.

'Do you not see how others suffer because of your obstinacy?'

'It is not my doing.'

'It is your doing. Do not allow any such thought as that to get into your mind, and assist the Devil in closing the door of your heart. They who are your friends are bound to you, and cannot separate themselves from you.'

'Who are my friends?'

'I am sorry you should ask that question, Linda.'

'I have no friends.'

'Linda, that is ungrateful to God, and thankless. I say nothing of myself.'

'You are my friend, but no one else.'

'Herr Molk is your friend, and has shown himself to be so. Jacob Heisse is your friend.' He, too, using such wisdom as he possessed, had recommended Linda to take the husband provided for her. 'Peter Steinmarc is your friend.'

'No, he is not,' said Linda.

'That is very wicked,—heinously wicked.' Whereupon Madame Staubach went towards the door for the purpose of bolting it, and Linda knew that this was preparatory to a prayer. Linda felt that it was impossible that she should fall on her knees and attempt to pray at this moment. What was the use of it? Sooner or later she must yield. She had no weapon with which to carry on the battle, whereas her aunt was always armed.

'Aunt Charlotte,' she said, suddenly, 'I will do what you want,—only not now; not quite yet. Let there be time for me to make myself ready for it.'

The dreaded visitation of that special prayer was at any rate arrested, and Madame Staubach graciously accepted Linda's assent as sufficient quittance at any rate for the evil words that had been spoken on that occasion. She was too wise to demand a more gracious acquiescence, and did not say a word then even in opposition to the earnest request which had been made for delay. She kissed her niece, and rejoiced as the woman rejoiced who had swept diligently and had found her lost piece. If Linda would at last take the right path, all former deviations from it should be as nothing. And Madame Staubach half-trusted, almost thought, that it could not be but that her own prayers should prevail at last. Linda indeed had twice before assented, and had twice retracted her word. But there had been causes. The young man had come and had prevailed, who surely would not come again, and who surely, if coming, would not prevail. And then Peter himself had misbehaved. It must now be Madame Staubach's care that there should arise no further stumbling-block. There were but two modes of taking this care at her disposal. She could watch Linda all the day, and she could reiterate her prayers with renewed diligence. On neither points would she be found lacking.

'And when shall be the happy day?' said Peter. On the occasion of his visit to the parlour subsequent to the scene which has just been described, Madame Staubach left the room for a while so that the two lovers might be together. Peter had been warned that it would be so, and had prepared, no doubt, his little speech.

'There will be no happy day,' said Linda.

'Don't say that, my dear.'

'I do say it. There will be no happy day for you or for me.'

'But we must fix a day, you know,' said Peter.

'I will arrange it with my aunt.' Then Linda got up and left the room. Peter Steinmarc attempted no further conversation with her, nor did Madame Staubach again endeavour to create any intercourse between them. It must come after marriage. It was clearly to her God's will that these two people should be married, and she could not but be right to leave the result to His wisdom. A day was named. With a simple nod of her head Linda agreed that she would become Peter's wife on the fifteenth of March; and she received visits from Herr Molk and from Jacob Heisse to congratulate her on her coming happiness.

CHAPTER XVI

THROUGHOUT February Linda never flinched. She hardly spoke at all except on matters of household business, but to them she was sedulously attentive. She herself insisted on understanding what legal arrangement was made about the house, and would not consent to sign the necessary document preparatory to her marriage till there was inserted in it a clause giving to her aunt a certain life-interest in the property in the event either of her marriage or of her death. Peter did his best to oppose this, as did also Madame Staubach herself; but Linda prevailed, and the clause was there. 'She would have to live with you whether or no,' said Herr Molk to the town-clerk. 'You couldn't turn the woman out into the street.' But Peter had wished to be master of his own house, and would not give up the point till much eloquence and authority had been used. He had come to wish with all his heart that he had never seen Linda Tressel or the red house; but he had gone so far that he could not retract. Linda never flinched, never uttered a word of complaint; sat silent while Peter was smoking, and awaited her doom. Once her aunt spoke to her about her feelings as a bride. 'You do love him, do you not, Linda?' said Madame Staubach. 'I do not love him,' Linda had replied. Then Madame Staubach dared to ask no further question, but prayed that the necessary affection might be given.

There were various things to be bought, and money

for the purpose was in a moderate degree forthcoming. Madame Staubach possessed a small hoard, which was now to be spent, and something she raised on her own little property. A portion of this was intrusted wholly to Linda, and she exercised care and discretion in its disposition. Linen for the house she purchased, and things needed for the rooms and the kitchen. But she would expend nothing in clothes for herself. When pressed on the subject by her aunt, she declared that her marriage would be one that required no finery. Her own condition and that of her proposed husband, she said, made it quite unnecessary. When she was told that Steinmarc would be offended by such exaggerated simplicity, she turned upon her aunt with such a look of scorn that Madame Staubach did not dare to say another word. Indeed at this time Madame Staubach had become almost afraid of her niece, and would sit watching the silent stern industry of the younger woman with something of awe. Could it be that there ever came over her heart a shock of regret for the thing she was doing? Was it possible that she should already be feeling remorse? If it was so with her, she turned herself to prayer, and believed that the Lord told her that she was right.

But there were others who watched, and spoke among themselves, and felt that the silent solemnity of Linda's mode of life was a cause for trembling. Max Bogen's wife had come to her father's house, and had seen Linda, and had talked to Tetchen, and had said at home that Linda was——mad. Her father had become frightened, and had refused to take any part in the matter. He acknowledged that he had given his advice in favour of the marriage, but he had done this merely as a matter of course,—to oblige his neighbour, Madame Staubach. He would have nothing more to do with it. When Fanny told him that she feared that Linda would lose her senses, he went into his workshop and busied himself with a great chair. But Tetchen was not so reticent. Tetchen said much to Madame Staubach;—so much that the unfortunate widow was nearly always on her knees, asking for help, asking in very truth for new gifts of obstinate persistency; and Tetchen also said much to Fanny Bogen.

'But what can we do, Tetchen?' asked Fanny.

'If I had my will,' said Tetchen, 'I would so handle him that he would be glad enough to be off his bargain. But you'll see they'll never live together as man and wife, —never for a day.'

They who said that Linda was mad at this time were probably half-right; but if so, her madness had shown itself in none of those forms which are held to justify interference by authority. There was no one in Nuremberg who could lock a woman up because she was silent; or could declare her to be unfit for marriage because she refused to buy wedding clothes. The marriage must go on. Linda herself felt that it must be accomplished. Her silence and her sternness were not now consciously used by her as means of opposing or delaying the coming ceremony, but simply betrayed the state of mind to which she was reduced. She counted the days and she counted the hours as a criminal counts them who sits in his cell and waits for the executioner. She knew, she thought she knew, that she would stand in the church and have her hand put into that of Peter Steinmarc; but what might happen after that she did not know.

She would stand at the altar and have her hand put into that of Peter Steinmarc, and she would be called his wife in sight of God and man. She spent hours in solitude attempting to realise the position with all its horrors. She never devoted a minute to the task of reconciling herself to it. She did not make one slightest endeavour towards teaching herself that after all it might be possible for her to live with the man as his companion in peace and quietness. She hated him with all the vigour of her heart, and she would hate him to the end. On that subject no advice, no prayer, no grace from heaven, could be of service to her. Satan, with all the horrors of hell, as they had been described to her, was preferable to the companionship of Peter Steinmarc. And yet she went on without flinching.

She went on without flinching till the night of the

tenth of March. Up to that time, from the day on which
she had last consented to her martyrdom, no idea of
escape had occurred to her. As she left her aunt on that
evening, Madame Staubach spoke to her. 'You should
at any rate pray for him,' said Madame Staubach. 'I
hope that you pray that this marriage may be for his
welfare.' How could she pray for him? And how could
she utter such a prayer as that? But she tried; and as she
tried, she reflected that the curse to him would be as
great as it was to her. Not only was she to be sacrificed,
but the miserable man was bringing himself also to utter
wretchedness. Unless she could die, there would be no
escape for him, as also there would be none for her. That
she should speak to him, touch him, hold intercourse
with him, was, she now told herself, out of the question.
She might be his servant, if he would allow her to be so
at a distance, but nothing more. Or it might be possible
that she should be his murderess! A woman who has
been taught by her religion that she is and must be a
child of the Evil One, may become guilty of what most
terrible crime you please without much increase of
damage to her own cause,—without much damage
according to her own views of life and death. Linda, as
she thought of it in her own chamber, with her eyes wide
open, looking into the dark night from out of her window,
declared to herself that in certain circumstances she
would certainly attempt to kill him. She shuddered and
shook till she almost fell from her chair. Come what
might, she would not endure the pressure of his caress.

Then she got up and resolved that she would even yet
make one other struggle to escape. It would not be true
of her to say that at this moment she was mad, but the
mixed excitement and terror of her position as she was
waiting her doom, joined to her fears, her doubts, and,
worse than all, her certainties as to her condition in the
sight of God, had almost unstrung her mind. She had
almost come to believe that the world was at its end, and
that the punishment of which she had heard so much
was already upon her. 'If this is to be a doom for ever,'
she said to herself, 'the God I have striven to love is very

cruel.' But then there came an exercise of reason which
told her that it could not be a doom for ever. It was clear
to her that there was much as yet within her own power
which could certainly not be so in that abode of the
unblessed to which she was to be summoned. There was
the window before her, with the silent river running
below; and she knew that she could throw herself from
it if she chose to put forth the power which she still
possessed. She felt that 'she herself might her quietus
make with a bare bodkin.' Why should she

> 'Fardels bear,
> To grunt and sweat under a weary life,
> But that the dread of something after life,
> The undiscovered country from whose bourne
> No traveller returns, puzzles the will,
> And makes us rather bear those ills we have
> Than fly to others that we know not of.'

Linda knew nothing of Hamlet, but the thought was
there, exact; and the knowledge that some sort of choice
was still open to her, if it were only the choice of sending
herself at once to a world different from this, a world in
which Peter Steinmarc would not be the avenger of
her life's wickedness, made her aware that even yet
something might be done.

On the following morning she was in the kitchen, as
was usual with her now, at an early hour, and made the
coffee for her aunt's breakfast, and for Peter's. Tetchen
was there also, and to Tetchen she spoke a word or two
in good humour. Tetchen said afterwards that she knew
that something was to happen, because Linda's manner
to her had been completely changed that morning. She
sat down with her aunt at eight, and ate a morsel of
bread, and endeavoured to swallow her coffee. She was
thinking at the time that it might be the case that she
would never see her aunt again. All the suffering that
she had endured at Madame Staubach's hands had never
quenched her love. Miserable as she had been made by
the manner in which this woman had executed the trust
which circumstances had placed in her hands, Linda
had hardly blamed her aunt even within her own bosom.

When with a frenzy of agony Madame Staubach would repeat prayer after prayer, extending her hands towards heaven, and seeking to obtain that which she desired by the painful intensity of her own faith, it had never occurred to Linda that in such proceedings she was ill-treated by her aunt. Her aunt, she thought, had ever shown to her all that love which a mother has for her child, and Linda in her misery was never ungrateful. As soon as the meal was finished she put on her hat and cloak, which she had brought down from her room, and then kissed her aunt.

'God bless you, my child,' said Madame Staubach, 'and enable you to be an affectionate and dutiful wife to your husband.' Then Linda went forth from the room and from the house, and as she went she cast her eyes around, thinking that it might be possible that she should never see them again.

Linda told no lie as she left her aunt, but she felt that she was acting a lie. It had been arranged between them, before she had entertained this thought of escaping from Nuremberg, that she should on this morning go out by herself and make certain purchases. In spite of the things that had been done, of Valcarm's visit to the upper storeys of the house, of the flight to Augsburg, of Linda's long protracted obstinacy and persistently expressed hatred for the man who was to be her husband, Madame Staubach still trusted her niece. She trusted Linda perhaps the more at this time from a feeling that she had exacted so much from the girl. When, therefore, Linda kissed her and went out, she had no suspicion on her mind; nor was any aroused till the usual dinner-hour was passed, and Linda was still absent. When Tetchen at one o'clock said something of her wonder that the fraulein had not returned, Madame Staubach had suggested that she might be with her friend Herr Molk. Tetchen knew what was the warmth of that friendship, and thought that such a visit was not probable. At three o'clock the postman brought a letter which Linda herself had dropped into the box of the post-office that morning, soon after leaving the house. She had known when, in ordinary course, it would be delivered. Should it lead by any misfortune to her discovery before she could escape, that she could not help. Even that, accompanied by her capture, would be as good a mode as any other of telling her aunt the truth. The letter was as follows:—

'*Thursday Night.*

'DEAREST AUNT,—I think you hardly know what are my sufferings. I truly believe that I have deserved them, but nevertheless they are insupportable. I cannot marry Peter Steinmarc. I have tried it, and cannot. The day is very near now; but were it to come nearer, I should go mad, or I should kill myself. I think that you do not know what the feeling is that has made me the most wretched of women since this marriage was first proposed to me. I shall go away to-morrow, and shall try to get to my uncle's house in Cologne. It is a long way off, and perhaps I shall never get there: but if I am to die on the road, oh, how much better will that be! I do not want to live. I have made you unhappy, and everybody unhappy, but I do not think that anybody has been so unhappy as I am. I shall give you a kiss as I go out, and you will think that it was the kiss of Judas; but I am not a Judas in my heart. Dear aunt Charlotte, I would have borne it if I could,—Your affectionate, but undutiful niece.

'LINDA TRESSEL.'

Undutiful! So she called herself; but had she not, in truth, paid duty to her aunt beyond that which one human being can in any case owe to another? Are we to believe that the very soul of the offspring is to be at the disposition of the parent? Poor Linda! Madame Staubach, when the letter was handed to her by Tetchen, sat aghast for a while, motionless, with her hands before her. 'She is off again, I suppose,' said Tetchen.

'Yes; she has gone.'

'It serves you right. I say it now, and I will say it. Why was she so driven?' Madame Staubach said never a word. Could she have had Linda back at the instant, just now, at this very moment, she would have yielded.

It was beginning to become apparent to her that God did not intend that her prayers should be successful. Doubtless the fault was with herself. She had lacked faith. Then as she sat there she began to reflect that it might be that she herself was not of the elect. What if, after all, she had been wrong throughout! 'Is anything to be done?' said Tetchen, who was still standing by her side.

'What ought I to do, Tetchen?'

'Wring Peter Steinmarc's neck,' said Tetchen. 'That would be the best thing.' Even this did not bring forth an angry retort from Madame Staubach. About an hour after that Peter came in. He had already heard that the bird had flown. Some messenger from Jacob Heisse's house had brought him the tidings to the town-hall.

'What is this?' said he. 'What is this? She has gone again.'

'Yes,' said Tetchen, 'she has gone again. What did you expect?'

'And Ludovic Valcarm is with her?'

'Ludovic Valcarm is not with her!' said Madame Staubach, with an expression of wrath which made him start a foot back from where he stood.

'Ah!' he exclaimed, when he had recovered himself, and reflected that he had no cause for fear, 'she is no better than she should be.'

'She is ten times too good for you. That is all that is the matter with her,' said Tetchen.

'I have done with her,—have done with her altogether,' said Peter, rubbing his hands together.

'I should think you have,' said Tetchen.

'Tell him to leave me,' said Madame Staubach, waving Peter away with her hand. Then Tetchen took the town-clerk by his arm, and led him somewhat roughly out of the room. So he shall disappear from our sight. No reader will now require to be told that he did not become the husband of Linda Tressel.

Madame Staubach did nothing and said nothing further on the matter that night. Tetchen indeed went up to the railway station, and found that Linda had

taken a ticket through to Mannheim, and had asked
questions there, openly, in reference to the boats from
thence down the Rhine. She had with her money
sufficient to take her to Cologne, and her aunt endeavoured to comfort herself with thinking that no
further evil would come of this journey than the cost,
and the rumours it would furnish. As to Peter Steinmarc,
that was now all over. If Linda would return, no further
attempt should be made. Tetchen said nothing on the
subject, but she herself was by no means sure that Linda
had no partner in her escape. To Tetchen's mind it was
so natural that there should be a partner.

Early on the following morning Madame Staubach
was closeted with Herr Molk in the panelled chamber of
the house in the Egidien Platz, seeking advice. 'Gone
again, is she?' said Herr Molk, holding up his hand.
'And that fellow is with her of course?'

'No, no, no!' exclaimed Madame Staubach.

'Are you sure of that! At any rate she must marry him
now, for nobody else will take her. Peter won't bite
again at that bait.' Then Madame Staubach was compelled to explain that all ideas of matrimony in respect
to her niece must be laid aside, and she was driven also
to confess that she had persevered too long in regard to
Peter Steinmarc. 'He certainly is a little rusty for such a
young woman as Linda,' said Herr Molk, confessing also
his part of the fault. At last he counselled Madame
Staubach that she could do nothing but follow her niece
to Cologne, as she had before followed her to Augsburg.
Such a journey would be very terrible to her. She had
not been in Cologne for years, and did not wish to see
again those who were there. But she felt that she had no
alternative, and she went.

CHAPTER XVII

For very many years no connection had been main-
tained between the two women who lived together in
Nuremberg, and their nearest relative, who was a half-
brother of Madame Staubach's, a lawyer, living in

Cologne. This uncle of Linda's was a Roman Catholic, and had on this account been shunned by Madame Staubach. Some slight intercourse there had been on matters of business, and thus it had come to pass that Linda knew the address of her uncle. But this was all that she knew, and knowing this only, she had started for Cologne. The reader will hardly require to be told that she had not gone in company with him who a few weeks since had been her lover. The reader, perhaps, will have understood Linda's character so thoroughly as to be convinced that, though she had submitted to be dragged out of her window by her lover, and carried away to Augsburg in the night, still it was not probable that she should again be guilty of such indiscretion as that. The lesson had not been in vain. If there be any reader who does not know Linda's character better than it was known to Herr Molk, or even to Tetchen, this story has been told in vain. All alone she started, and all alone she made the entire journey. Long as it was, there was no rest for her on the way. She went by a cheap and slow train, and on she went through the long day and the long night, and on through the long day again. She did not suffer with the cold as she had suffered on that journey to Augsburg, but the weariness of the hours was very great, and the continuation of the motion oppressed her sorely. Then joined to this suffering was the feeling that she was going to a strange world in which no one would receive her kindly. She had money to take her to Cologne, but she would have none to bring her back again. It seemed to her as she went that there could be no prospect to her returning to a home which she had disgraced so thoroughly.

At Mannheim she found that she was obliged to wait over four hours before the boat started. She quitted the railway a little after midnight, and she was told that she was to be on board before five in the morning. The night was piercing cold, though never so cold as had been that other night; and she was dismayed at the thought of wandering about in that desolate town. Some one, however, had compassion on her, and she was taken to a small inn, in which she rested on a bed without removing her clothes. When she rose in the morning, she walked down to the boat without a word of complaint, but she found that her limbs were hardly able to carry her. An idea came across her mind that if the people saw that she was ill they would not take her upon the boat. She crawled on, and took her place among the poorer passengers before the funnels. For a considerable time no one noticed her, as she sat shivering in the cold morning air on a damp bench. At last a market-woman going down to Mayence asked her a question. Was she ill? Before they had reached Mayence she had told her whole story to the market-woman. 'May God temper the wind for thee, my shorn lamb!' said the market-woman to Linda, as she left her; 'for it seems that thou hast been shorn very close.' By this time, with the assistance of the woman, she had found a place below in which she could lie down, and there she remained till she learned that the boat had reached Cologne. Some one in authority on board the vessel had been told that she was ill; and as they had reached Cologne also at night, she was allowed to remain on board till the next morning. With the early dawn she was astir, and the full daylight of the March morning was hardly perfect in the heavens when she found herself standing before the door of a house in the city, to which she had been brought as being the residence of her uncle.

She was now, in truth, so weak and ill that she could hardly stand. Her clothes had not been off her back since she left Nuremberg, nor had she come prepared with any change of raiment. A woman more wretched, more disconsolate, on whose shoulders the troubles of this world lay heavier, never stood at an honest man's door to beg admittance. If only she might have died as she crawled through the streets!

But there she was, and she must make some petition that the door might be opened for her. She had come all the way from Nuremberg to this spot, thinking it possible that in this spot alone she might receive succour; and now she stood there, fearing to raise the knocker on the door. She was a lamb indeed, whose fleece had been shorn very close; and the shearing had been done all in the sacred name of religion! It had been thought necessary that the vile desires of her human heart should be crushed within her bosom, and the crushing had brought her to this. She looked up in her desolation at the front of the house. It was a white, large house, as belonging to a moderately prosperous citizen, with two windows on each side of the door, and five above, and then others again above them. But there seemed to be no motion within it, nor was there any one stirring along the street. Would it not be better, she thought, that she should sit for a while and wait upon the door-step? Who has not known that frame of mind in which any postponement of the thing dreaded is acceptable?

But Linda's power of postponement was very short. She had hardly sunk on to the step, when the door was opened, and the necessity for explaining herself came upon her. Slowly and with pain she dragged herself on to her feet, and told the suspicious servant, who stood filling the aperture of the doorway, that her name was Linda Tressel, and that she had come from Nuremberg. She had come from the house of Madame Staubach at Nuremberg. Would the servant be kind enough to tell Herr Grüner that Linda Tressel, from Madame Staubach's house in Nuremberg, was at his door? She claimed no kindred then, feeling that the woman might take such claim as a disgrace to her master. When she was asked to call again later, she looked piteously into the woman's face, and said that she feared she was too ill to walk away.

Before the morning was over she was in bed, and her uncle's wife was at her bedside, and there had been fair-haired cousins in her room, creeping in to gaze at her with their soft blue eyes, touching her with their young soft hands, and calling her Cousin Linda with their soft voices. It seemed to her that she could have died happily, so happily, then, if only they might have been allowed to stand round her bed, and still to whisper and still to touch her. But they had been told that they might only

just see their new cousin and then depart,— because the
new cousin was ill. The servant at the front door had
doubted her, as it is the duty of servants to doubt in such
cases; but her uncle had not doubted, and her uncle's
wife, when she heard the story, wept over her, and told
her that she should be at rest.

Linda told her story from the first to the last. She told
everything,—her hatred for the one man, her love for the
other; her journey to Augsburg. 'Ah, dear, dear, dear,'
said aunt Grüner when this was told to her. 'I know how
wicked I have been,' said Linda, sorrowing. 'I do not
say that you have been wicked, my dear, but you have
been unfortunate,' said aunt Grüner. And then Linda
went on to tell her, as the day so much dreaded by her
drew nearer and nearer, as she came to be aware that,
let her make what effort she would, she could not bring
herself to be the man's wife,—that the horror of it was
too powerful for her,—she resolved at the last moment
that she would seek the only other relative in the world
of whom she knew even the name. Her aunt Grüner
thoroughly commended her for this, saying, however,
that it would have been much better that she should have
made the journey at some period earlier in her troubles.
'Aunt Charlotte does not seem to be a very nice sort of
woman to live with,' said aunt Grüner. Then Linda,
with what strength she could, took Madame Staubach's
part. 'She always thought that she was doing right,' said
Linda, solemnly. 'Ah, that comes of her religion,' said
aunt Grüner. 'We think differently, my dear. Thank
God, we have got somebody to tell us what we ought to
do and what we ought not to do.' Linda was not strong
enough to argue the question, or to remind her aunt that
this somebody, too, might possibly be wrong.

Linda Tressel was now happier than she had remembered herself to have been since she was a child, though
ill, so that the doctor who came to visit her could only
shake his head and speak in whispers to aunt Grüner.
Linda herself, perceiving how it was with the doctor,—
knowing that there were whispers though she did not
hear them, and shakings of the head though she did not

see them,—told her aunt with a smile that she was contented to die. Her utmost hope, the extent of her wishes, had been to escape from the extremity of misery to which she had been doomed. She had thought often, she said, as she had been making that journey, that her strength would not serve her to reach the house of her relative. 'God,' she said, 'had been very good to her, and she was now contented to go.'

Madame Staubach arrived at Cologne four days after her niece, and was also welcomed at her brother's house. But the welcome accorded to her was not that which had been given to Linda. 'She has been driven very nearly to death's door among you,' said the one aunt to the other. To Linda Madame Staubach was willing to own that she had been wrong, but she could make no such acknowledgment to the wife of her half-brother,—to a benighted Papist. 'I have endeavoured to do my duty by my niece,' said Madame Staubach, 'asking the Lord daily to show me the way.' 'Pshaw!' said the other woman. 'Your always asking the way, and never knowing it, will end in her death. She will have been murdered by your prayers.' This was very terrible, but for Linda's sake it was borne.

There was nothing of reproach either from Linda to her aunt or from Madame Staubach to her niece, nor was the name of Peter Steinmarc mentioned between them for many days. It was, indeed, mentioned but once again by poor Linda Tressel. For some weeks, for nearly a month, they all remained in the house of Herr Grüner, and then Linda was removed to apartments in Cologne, in which all her earthly troubles were brought to a close. She never saw Nuremberg again, or Tetchen, who had been faithful at least to her, nor did she ever even ask the fate of Ludovic Valcarm. His name Madame Staubach never dared to mention; and Linda was silent, thinking always that it was a name of offence. But when she had been told that she must die,—that her days were indeed numbered, and that no return to Nuremberg was possible for her,—she did speak a word of Peter Steinmarc. 'Tell him, aunt Charlotte, from me,' she said, 'that I prayed for him when I was dying, and that I forgave him. You know, aunt Charlotte, it was impossible that I should marry him. A woman must not marry a man whom she does not love.' Madame Staubach did not venture to say a word in her own justification. She did not dare even to recur to the old tenets of her fierce religion, while Linda still lived. She was cowed, and contented herself with the offices of a nurse by the sickbed of the dying girl. She had been told by her sister-in-law that she had murdered her niece. Who can say what were the accusations brought against her by the fury of her own conscience?

Every day the fair-haired cousins came to Linda's bedside, and whispered to her with their soft voices, and looked at her with their soft eyes, and touched her with their soft hands. Linda would kiss their plump arms and lean her head against them, and would find a very paradise of happiness in this late revelation of human love. As she lay a-dying she must have known that the world had been very hard to her, and that her aunt's teaching had indeed crushed her,—body as well as spirit. But she made no complaint; and at last, when the full summer had come, she died at Cologne in Madame Staubach's arms.

During those four months at Cologne the zeal of Madame Staubach's religion had been quenched, and she had been unable to use her fanaticism, even towards herself. But when she was alone in the world the fury of her creed returned. 'With faith you shall move a mountain,' she would say, 'but without faith you cannot live.' She could never trust her own faith, for the mountain would not be moved.

A small tombstone in the Protestant burying-ground at Cologne tells that Linda Tressel, of Nuremberg, died in that city on the 20th of July 1863, and that she was buried in that spot.

THE END